It Was All a Part of Her Fantasy . . .

In a silent underwater ballet they moved through the dimness. He was all grace and flow, but so strong, so male. She felt the long, lean length of him as his lips brushed hers.

This couldn't really be happening. Maybe she'd fallen asleep floating there near the lilies. When she had smiled at him, she'd seen the longing in his eyes. Longing and need. Longing and tenderness. "Jared—"

His finger across her lips silenced her. "Me Tarzan, you Jane," he whispered as his hand moved from her mouth down across her throat to her breast.

NORA POWERS

taught English at the college level while working on her Ph.D. A prolific writer, she is the author of some 500 pieces of children's verse, 58 short stories, 9 novels and various newspaper articles. She has been a published author for the last twenty years and reports, "I don't even recall how I started writing, I was so young."

Dear Reader:

Silhouette has always tried to give you exactly what you want. When you asked for increased realism, deeper characterization and greater length, we brought you Silhouette Special Editions. When you asked for increased sensuality, we brought you Silhouette Desire. Now you ask for books with the length and depth of Special Editions, the sensuality of Desire, but with something else besides, something that no one else offers. Now we bring you SILHOUETTE INTIMATE MOMENTS, true romance novels, longer than the usual, with all the depth that length requires. More sensuous than the usual, with characters whose maturity matches that sensuality. Books with the ingredient no one else has tapped: excitement.

There is an electricity between two people in love that makes everything they do magic, larger than life—and this is what we bring you in SILHOUETTE INTIMATE MOMENTS. Look for them this May, wherever you buy books.

These books are for the woman who wants more than she has ever had before. These books are for you. As always, we look forward to your comments and suggestions. You can write to me at the address below:

Karen Solem
Editor-in-Chief
Silhouette Books
P.O. Box 769
New York, N.Y. 10019

NORA POWERS
Time Stands Still

Silhouette Desire

Published by Silhouette Books New York

America's Publisher of Contemporary Romance

Other Silhouette Books by Nora Powers

Affairs of the Heart
Design for Love
Promise Me Tomorrow
Dream of the West

SILHOUETTE BOOKS, a Simon & Schuster Division of
GULF & WESTERN CORPORATION
1230 Avenue of the Americas, New York, N.Y. 10020

Copyright © 1983 by Nora Powers

Distributed by Pocket Books

ISBN: 0-671-45063-8

First Silhouette Books printing April, 1983

10 9 8 7 6 5 4 3 2 1

America's Publisher of Contemporary Romance

Printed in the U.S.A.

for William

1

~~~~~~~~~~~~~~~~

Oh, darling!" Libby Collins moaned softly in her sleep, her pale blond head turning restlessly on the crumpled pillow. "Jared!" His lips were on hers, warm persuasive lips that made her body long for his closeness. She could feel him so distinctly, the long, lean length of him, the hard-muscled body of a man who did heavy physical labor.

She tasted the sweetness of his kisses, savored his caressing hands. Every nerve ending in her skin was working overtime, sending sensations of desire throughout her yearning body. She felt his arms gather her close, felt the hardness of his chest crushing the softness of her swelling breasts. How wonderful it was to belong to Jared, to feel his heart beating under her hand, to run her fingers through his thick, brown hair. She loved him; she loved Jared Harper with all her body and soul.

His hands moved, positioning her. In another wonderful moment they would be one, one in the ultimate union.

The roar of a motor outside the open window jolted Libby abruptly awake. For a single dazed moment she thought the dream was still reality, and her hand reached out to touch him. But even before it encountered empty space she knew the truth. Jared Harper was not sharing her bed. She was alone in it, alone as she had been for so many, many nights.

"Damn him!" Libby said to the empty room. "Why does he keep coming back to haunt me?"

She threw aside the rumpled covers and stared at the dark ceiling. Jared's presence might have been a dream, brought into flowering by her unconscious, but her longing for him was very real. Deep within her throbbed an insistent need.

She flopped over on her stomach and pummeled the pillow. This was stupid. Dreaming about Jared when she hadn't seen him for seven long years.

Sighing, she rolled over onto her back again and willed herself to forget. Seven years ago she'd been eighteen. Young and foolish, to be sure. But who wouldn't have fallen madly in love with Jared Harper? At twenty-three he represented the mystery and glamour of an "older" man. Knocking about the oil fields since he was thirteen had made him tough and hard-shelled, but with her he had been all tenderness, as amazed as she at the wondrous feeling that grew between them.

She remembered the first time she'd seen him. Against her darkened eyelids the picture appeared in clear colors. It had been one of those hot Texas days, and Libby, off school for the summer, had taken her car and gone out to the fields. She had never been able to understand her mother's abhorrence of the oil fields. Libby thought them fascinating, exciting places. She liked the smell of oil and the grins of the tough workmen. Every one knew she was Bob Collins's girl, so they were careful with their language. She liked the fields, liked the atmosphere, liked to watch the men at work.

But on this day it was one particular man who drew her eyes. Tall and lean, with chestnut-brown hair that curled out from under his hard hat, he paused in adjusting something, paused long enough to give her a thorough going-over from green-gray eyes. When his glance met hers for a brief moment, Libby flushed and turned away. His look had been tough and appraising. She probably ought to resent it. But she knew she didn't.

She tried not to pay too much attention to the man, but she couldn't seem to control her eyes. They kept going back to him, going back to the hard, brown face and the gloved hands that moved so deftly. When he finished tightening the bolts and walked away, she felt a strange sense of loss. Almost immediately her feet took her in the same direction. As he settled down in the scant shade of a truck, she paused beside him. "You're new, aren't you?" she said, unconsciously putting a lot of warmth into her smile.

"Yep." His answer was short, but his eyes lingered on her long, smooth legs.

"You from around here?" Libby asked. "I don't remember seeing you before."

"You haven't," he said. "I just blew into town."

Excitement throbbed through Libby. "Going to stay long?"

His eyes met hers with a long, lingering look that made her feel all queer inside. "Maybe. Ain't made up my mind yet."

"I hope you do," she said, her mouth gone suddenly dry.

"Unh huh."

His look was almost an insult, and Libby flushed. She didn't know why she was acting so strangely. Boys had been asking her for dates for a long time. She'd been kissed, too. But nothing like this had ever happened to her—the strange pounding of her heart and the heat that seemed to suffuse her when she felt his eyes on her.

This realization made her even more nervous and she smiled timidly. "Sorry to bother you," she mumbled and moved hurriedly away. She was sure his eyes were still on her and suddenly her shorts and top seemed far too scanty. She tried to walk without swinging her hips and as soon as possible she managed to put something solid between herself and the man.

For the rest of the afternoon she avoided him,

talking instead to the workers who knew her, inquiring about a wife here, a child there. It was about 3 o'clock when she headed back for the car. She fought with herself: She couldn't stand it if he caught her looking at him again. But she could not resist one last glance. Fortunately he was engrossed in his work and didn't notice her. Again Libby felt the strange sensations assailing her body. What kind of power did this man have that he could make her feel like melting just by looking at her? Determinedly she turned back toward her car. It wouldn't do to be late to dinner.

She opened her car door and gasped. On the front seat, anchored by a piece of scrap iron, lay a crumpled sheet of paper. Libby pushed it to one side and scrambled into the car. Trying to keep a carefree face, she waved at her friends as she drove away.

She put several miles between herself and the rig before she halted the car. Her breath was heavy in her throat, and her hands trembled as she reached for the paper. She opened it with shaky fingers. There was nothing on it but numbers. Libby's heart seemed to skip a beat. It was a phone number. *His* phone number. She knew that as well as she knew her own name.

She started the little car and sped off toward the city. She would not call him, of course. How dare he think such a thing. And yet . . . Just thinking about him, about the sinews in his bare brown arms, about the damp T-shirt clinging to his muscular chest, about the dusty blue jeans molding his lean hips—just thinking about him made her heart pound painfully, and that terrible longing started up in her again.

She wasn't sure exactly what she longed *for,* but she knew it had to do with him, with feeling those strong arms around her, with being held close to that lean body. All the way home she was firmly convinced that she would never use that phone number. She did not throw it away, though. She had never been one to litter, she told herself as she stuffed it into her purse.

She could have discarded it, of course. The figures were engraved in her brain. They burned there through dinner while her socialite mother related the usual events of her day and Libby and her father nodded at the appropriate moments. The meal was over, finally, and Libby escaped to her room to wander around and stare at herself in the mirror. What had he seen, that arrogant roustabout, when he looked her over? Did he like her breasts? She regarded them anxiously. They were high and firm. He must have seen that. She had looked nice. She knew it.

And he . . . He had looked dangerous. She threw herself down on the white-ruffled bed. He had looked very dangerous. This was a man she was dealing with, not a schoolboy with fumbling fingers. If that man ever got his hands on her—Libby shivered—he would know exactly what to do. His eyes had told her that. He knew about life, Libby thought. He knew because he had lived it.

She got to her feet and walked over to the window, looking out through the lacy white curtains at Mama's expensively landscaped garden. But Libby didn't see the flowers. She saw a lean, dark face. Was that what made him seem dangerous? she wondered. That he had lived?

Her breath caught in her throat, and suddenly she knew. She knew with crystal clarity what it was that drew her to him. He knew about life—and love. He *knew* and she wanted him to teach *her*.

Libby put her hands to her burning face. No boy in school had ever affected her like this. And there had been plenty who'd been interested in her. She'd even dated a few. Let them kiss her. But she hadn't let any of them go further. The feeling had not been there, the feeling she knew instinctively *would* be when the right man came along. And the feeling was there now, so strong that she felt suffocated by it. This was the man she'd been waiting for. Blindly she turned to the phone and dialed.

It rang six times, and her heart began to slow its frantic pounding. Then his voice came across the wire, strong and vibrant as the man himself. "Hello."

"Hello." She managed the one word and then fell silent.

"I thought I got your message," he said. "Where do we meet?"

For a long second Libby's tongue wouldn't work. "I—I don't know. My folks . . . I can't."

He laughed. "Don't worry, baby. I'll fix it. Call me back tomorrow night. And listen, kid, next time you come out to the field don't make yourself so obvious. One or two looks would have let me know where you stand."

"But—" Libby stammered. "I've never—" She stopped, suddenly aware that a man like this would not believe her to be innocent.

"Got to go," he said. "Catch you later."

She hung up the phone, her face burning more than ever, her body heated with the thought of him. This whole thing was crazy. She couldn't do anything like this. It was insane. She would forget the whole idea, put it out of her mind.

But the next night found her reaching for the phone with trembling fingers.

"Hello," he said gruffly, and her heart jumped up in her throat.

"Hello. I . . . You said to call—"

"Listen, jail bait, I don't know what your game is, but leave me out of it."

The harshness of his voice tore at her, left her feeling lacerated. "What—what do you mean?" she stammered.

"I mean I've been cued in. Your little act was observed by several guys. At least two of 'em took pains to warn me not to mess around with the big man's daughter. He wouldn't like it, and neither would they. Boy, you've sure done a snow job on them guys. They talk like you were pure as snow. They couldn't have seen the looks you gave me."

"I never—" Libby's lips trembled. "I didn't know what I was doing. That is, I just liked you. And I wanted to get to know you."

"Yeah. Sure. Like the fox likes chickens. Listen, kid, I don't need trouble."

"I don't want to get you in trouble. Really. It's true. I just—wanted to get to know you."

"What for?"

"I . . . You look like you know. About things. About life."

"I know about life," he said harshly. "It stinks."

14

"But . . . Don't you believe in love?" The words were out before she could stop them.

"Love! By damn!"

Libby felt the tears rising. "What's so awful about love?" she demanded.

His laugh was short and harsh. "Not awful, kid. Just stupid."

She swallowed over the lump in her throat. "I don't see why. Love is important."

His laughter was loud and strong. "Not to me. You're the craziest little broad I've ever seen. Whatta you want from me anyway?"

"Could we maybe go out? To a movie or something?"

"You're kidding. I haven't gone to a movie with a girl since I was fifteen."

"Oh." Libby could think of nothing more to say. For the first time in her life she felt really weak and helpless. "What do you want me to do?" she whispered.

"Forget about me," he snapped. "Stay in your own neat little world. Don't come around messing up mine." And the line went dead.

She tried to do as he said, tried to forget him. But the field drew her like a magnet. She couldn't stay away, and once there she couldn't keep her eyes off him.

It took several weeks, but finally she found another crumpled piece of paper bearing his number. "Okay," he said when she called. "We'll go to a movie. But you've got to promise. Keep away from the field. I need this job."

She agreed, and she kept her word. She didn't

need to go there after that. For she gave him her phone number and he started to call her.

They saw each other three times a week for a month, and all he did was hold her hand. Libby was happy to be with him, happy just to be able to talk to him, to discover that under his gruff exterior lay a kind, gentle man. He must have been that—not to have availed himself of what she so clearly offered.

Then one night he saw her to her car and shut the door between them. "Listen, kid," he said through the open window. "You're too young. This has got to stop. I can't handle it anymore. If you come out to the job and gawk at me till I get fired, OK, then that's that. But I'm not made of iron. I've got feelings, too."

"Do you, Jared?" she said softly. "Tell me about them."

He ignored her. "You go home," he ordered harshly. "Go home and wait for some nice guy to come along. He will. Goodbye."

She watched him walk away, watched him quite calmly. She watched him climb into his battered jeep and drive off. Then she waited ten minutes and drove to his house. It was a little place; he had never allowed her inside. But tonight she was determined. It was not just his physical attraction that had drawn her to him. There was a quiet, determined strength to him, a basic goodness that had not been defiled by those years of rough living.

She parked the little car partway down the street and walked up to the door. She did not tremble; she was perfectly calm. She knew exactly what she was doing.

The door opened. "What the hell?" He had taken

16

off his shirt and his chest was revealed in the light from the street lamp.

She stepped inside and pushed the door shut behind her. "Please, Jared," she begged. "Don't send me away. Please! I need you."

"You've gotta go," he began, but she threw herself against him and raised herself on tiptoe. With a muffled curse he folded her in his arms. It was ecstasy. It was even better than she had imagined. She clung to him, raising her mouth hungrily for his kisses, her fingers digging into his hard shoulders.

His kiss was long and almost savage, a primitive release of the desire long pent up inside him. He was breathing heavily when he finished, but he tried to push her away. "Get out of here. While you still can."

She shook her head. "No, Jared. I'm not leaving. You want me. You know it. I know it. You wanted me that first day. And I want you."

"You're just a kid," he said, his breath coming in gasps. "An innocent kid."

She took one of his brown hands in hers and put it on her breast. "I'm a woman, Jared. A woman who wants you."

He gave into her then, as she had known he must. She had meant to stay until he did.

"All right," he said. "You win. But don't blame me for this later on. Remember, you started it."

She smiled at him, her eyes luminous. "I'll remember, Jared."

And so he had led her to his bed, neatly made, in a room so sparsely furnished that it gave no indication of his personality at all. And there he made love to her.

In spite of his own very obvious need, he took a

long time, caressing her body tenderly, his hands cupping each quivering breast and stroking the long curves of her hips and thighs before his mouth bent to the same task.

Libby could scarcely breathe for joy. This was it. This was what she had waited so long for. She held back nothing, offering herself to him fully and freely.

"It's gonna hurt," he said as he prepared to make love to her. "But only for a minute. After that it'll be great."

And he was right. The momentary stab of pain was gone almost immediately, and her body began to respond to the feel of his. He paused more than once, delaying his own release to use his hands and mouth so that when she finally heard his sharp exclamation of fulfillment it was mingled with her own moans of joy.

Tears spilled down Libby's face there in the lonely darkness. Yes, Jared Harper had been her first man. But she could not let him be her last.

She got up from the rumpled bed and went to bathe her face in cool water. She had to get back to sleep. Jared was gone—out of her life for seven long years. She sighed. She could remember him so clearly. It seemed that sometimes she could remember every time they had made love. She couldn't, of course. There had been too many. But she could remember her wedding day. The quick trip across the border, the equally quick Mexican marriage and the wrath of her parents.

But she had always fought for what she wanted. And she fought for Jared, for the right to be his wife. And when they had settled in his little house together, she had thought it the beginning of heaven.

Actually, it was the beginning of hell. Jared got transferred to another field, refusing to let her follow him there. He came home every weekend dead tired. Then things had gone from bad to worse. There were arguments over money; he didn't want her to take anything from her parents. More arguments because he was too tired on weekends to go places with her and she was bored with spending so much time alone. Even her mother's companionship, surprising since she had never before thought Libby worthy of it, couldn't fill the gap.

And the arguments grew even worse, culminating in that last horrible row when she had accused him of seeing another woman and, enraged at his counter-accusation, had threatened to leave him. But it was he who had done the leaving, stomping out in a rage and not coming back. In the morning she had thrown her clothes into a bag and gone back to her parents.

So Jared had left her life. Her parents had handled all the divorce proceedings, glad to rid the family of the interloper.

Libby sighed and moved to the window. She looked out, unseeing, at Houston Street, rubbing tiredly at her temples. For seven long years she had tried to get him out of her system, to forget him.

Her fingers played absently with the strings of her nightgown. Seven years. She'd gone to college, sticking to her guns when her parents found out about her geology major, insisting on finishing even when they withdrew their support, learning how to look for oil. The oil fields still had their lure for her. It was in her blood, she supposed.

And she liked her job. She liked World Wide Exploration. She'd had other offers when she graduated. Her grades were very good and she knew her stuff. But she'd chosen World Wide—chosen it, she admitted to herself, because Jared Harper was employed by the company. He worked overseas. In the Sumatra-Malaysia area, she had read. Yes, she knew she had joined World Wide because of that, because of Jared Harper. He was in her blood, too. She couldn't seem to escape him.

He had haunted her through the long years at school, through the split with her parents and the near poverty afterward. He had stood between her and every man who had tried to love her. His face and his body were so imprinted on her senses that no other man's kisses, no other man's caresses, could erase them.

With a deep sigh, Libby moved back toward the bed. She knew, really, why Jared was so much on her mind tonight. It was because tomorrow was the day that the assignment for the Sumatra trip would be made, the assignment she wanted so badly she could taste it. If she could get that assignment, she had told herself, if she could go to Sumatra and meet Jared Harper face to face, if she could confront the man himself and destroy the image she'd had of him during her adolescence, maybe then she could wipe away the childish memories of first love by facing the bitter truth. Maybe then she could build a decent future for herself.

With another sigh, she eased herself back into the rumpled bed. Morning would have to come eventually.

2

~~~~~~~~~~~~~~

A month later, Libby leaned toward the window of
the great jet. Beneath her lay the city of Singapore,
and down there somewhere was Jared Harper. Before
the day was over she would face him once more. She
shifted anxiously in her seat. The trip had been long
and tiring, and that, coupled with the state of her
nerves because of the impending meeting with Jared,
had left her feeling limp and exhausted. She frowned.
She simply had to pull herself together. After all, she
had survived the past month, beginning with her
superior's questions concerning her willingness to
undertake a difficult and strenuous assignment in the

heart of the Sumatran jungle and ending with hectic days of packing. Her passport, fortunately, had been in order. World Wide's employees were supposed to be prepared.

Libby pushed a stray wisp of hair back from her forehead. The plane was actually quite cool, but she felt almost feverish. What would the years have done to Jared? Would he still be so breathtakingly handsome? Would he be fat and bald? A nervous laugh fluttered in her throat. She couldn't even begin to imagine a Jared like that. He had always taken good care of his body. No, he would still be dark and virile, tanned by the tropic sun. And cruel. There was no doubt he would be cruel.

The last words he had said to her still burned in her brain. "Go ahead," he had yelled. "Go home to your precious mother. You never wanted a husband. You wanted a toy! Well, I've had it! I'm through. Go play your tricks on some other fool, baby. I only hope he's smarter than I was."

Rage had enveloped her then, and it returned to her now. He always seemed to think the worst of people. How long she had had to work to persuade him to run off and marry her. But she had thought he loved her. He'd even said it, and she didn't think he'd lie about a thing like that.

But, evidently, her mother had been right. Libby frowned. How she'd hated those little acid hints her mother dropped so often. Had Jared bought her this? Had they done that? And, of course, he bought her very little. They were saving for their own home. That had been very important to him.

Libby sighed, and the anger receded. It had been

important to her, too. It was just that she got so bored, left alone through the long weeks, got so bored she had to do something. And shopping had filled the gap. If only she had not been so used to getting her own way—or if Jared hadn't got transferred to that distant field and refused to let her go with him. She supposed he wanted to think of her as safe. She could see that now. But then all she could see was that she was desperately alone, that she needed to be with him.

The plane circled over the city. Libby saw the sun sparkling on distant glass. Skyscrapers reached upward from the great city that housed most of the country's two million people. Down there lay a whole new experience—a country built by people of many cultures and religions.

She would think about this new assignment, think about the adventure of being in a foreign place. There was no need to concentrate on memories of the bad times with Jared; the hateful words they had flung at each other were hard enough to forget. No probing was needed to bring forth those cruel and painful moments. They would be quite ready when she summoned them. But now she bent once more toward the window.

This was her first assignment outside the States, and it was exciting to think of what awaited her down there. It would be pleasant if she could find the time to do a little sightseeing. She would at least find the time to buy herself a souvenir or two. What she would really like was an old ivory or jade carving, but she had read enough to know that with her limited expertise she was far more likely to buy a fake than a genuine antique. Libby smiled. It really didn't matter. All she wanted was a token of this exotic place.

The seat belt sign had been turned on for some time, and Libby checked her belt and sat back. It was not the landing of the plane that frightened her, she knew. It was the prospect of meeting Jared again—after all these years.

Some minutes later Libby stood alone, patiently waiting for her baggage. The airport did not make her nervous. She had been in many different ones over the years. But she did find it intriguing. The people looked so different. Here was a dark-skinned, graceful Indian woman in a lovely silken sari, with a jewel in her nose; there was a Chinese woman, slim and supple in her long, tight cheongsam with the modest, high collar and daring slit up the side. Libby looked for dark Malaysian women in the sarongs she had read about, but found that most of the women around her wore Western dress—blue jeans and sneakers on the young women, dresses or pantsuits on the middle-aged.

Libby grabbed her bag as it came off the moving roundel. Well, here she was in Singapore. And there seemed to be no one to meet her. At that moment a voice came over the loudspeaker, a soft Asian voice with an unmistakable British accent. "Miss Libby Collins to the Merpati Airlines Desk. Miss Libby Collins."

At last, Libby thought, making her way through the crowd. But the man standing beside the Merpati desk was not Jared Harper. He was tall enough and his shoulders were broad, but his hair was sandy-colored rather than dark and his eyes were a warm brown.

"Libby Collins?" he asked.

Libby nodded. "That's me."

"Nick Brent. I'm part of the team you'll be working with. Sorry I'm late. Been out in the jungle for so long I forgot to allow for city traffic. Hope you haven't been waiting long."

Libby shook her head. "Not long at all. I just got my baggage."

Nick Brent's eyes went to the single bag. "You travel light."

Libby laughed. She was feeling a little giddy now that the meeting with Jared had been postponed. "That's one of the first things I learned. Take only what's essential." She smiled. "The front office said you had all the equipment."

Nick nodded. "We do."

"Fine. Then I have everything I need. Is the rest of the team here?" She hoped her voice had shown only normal interest.

Nick picked up her bag. "Tim got in this morning. Haven't seen the boss yet. Let's go."

As Libby followed him through the crowds, she tried to rally her thoughts. If only she could think of this as just another assignment. If only Jared did not fill her every waking thought. And sleeping ones, too.

Nick Brent seemed to know his way around the city. He called them a cab and helped her inside. After the heat of the outdoors Libby was grateful. The plane's air conditioning had not helped to prepare her for this heavy, wet heat.

"Ever been here before?" Nick asked.

Libby summoned a smile. "No. It looks like a fascinating place."

Nick grinned. "I suppose so. Most women like it."

"Why?"

His grin widened. "I guess because they're always looking for bargains and Change Alley is like one giant sale."

"Change Alley?"

"The regular marketplace, so to speak. You've got to see it. But never buy anything at the asking price."

"Why not?" asked Libby, her eyes going to the crowded street outside the car.

"Because this is an Oriental nation," Nick said briskly. "And its people love to bargain. You spoil their fun if you don't."

"Have you been here long?"

"In and out for the last couple years," he said. "Singapore's an R and R stop for all kinds of crews." He smiled ruefully. "When you come out of that jungle, you're more ready for rest than recreation. I've been lots of places. None of them are worse than the jungle we're going to."

"What hotel are we at?" Libby asked. She had not given much consideration to the jungle and she did not want to now. All her thoughts had been on Jared.

"The Singapore Hilton," Nick said. "World Wide treats its crews good. Real good."

"I wouldn't have thought otherwise," said Libby, turning back to the window. "How big is this city?" she asked curiously.

"The whole thing's about the size of Chicago," Nick replied. "I think it covers about twenty-five square miles."

Libby sighed. "It's exciting to see new places, but I'm afraid jet lag is catching up to me."

"You'd better get to bed early tonight," Nick said. "Unfortunately, our schedule doesn't allow for things like jet lag."

"I'll be fine," Libby insisted. "I'm strong as a horse."

Nick shook his head. "'Fraid horses don't do so well in the jungle."

His look was rather skeptical, and Libby forced herself to smile widely. "Don't worry about me. I'll be fine."

He looked as though he were about to make another comment, but just then the cab drew up to the hotel. The Singapore Hilton was another tower of glass and concrete. Libby couldn't help thinking that Singapore seemed to be a very modern city.

Nick opened the door for her, and Libby almost drew back. Here in the city the heat was a palpable physical presence, striking her almost like a blow.

Nick grinned at her as he extracted her bag. "It's the humidity," he said. "You'll get used to it. Anyhow, the hotel's air conditioned. Why don't you take a cool shower, get settled in your room. Then we'll go up to the Tradewinds for a little something cool."

"The Tradewinds?"

Nick nodded. "It's a nice little bar next to Hin's Heavenly Cookhouse. Up on the roof. There's a pool up there, too."

Libby smiled. "World Wide does treat us well."

Nick shrugged. "We deserve it."

An hour later, wearing a noncrushable dress of sea-green gauze, Libby looked down at the pink-fruit concoction in front of her and took a deep breath. Tim, a grizzled veteran of numerous expeditions, was eyeing her suspiciously from across the table. "You're really a geologist," he said.

"Really," Libby replied.

"Never seen a lady geologist before," Tim said. "Didn't imagine you'd look like this."

Libby put warmth in her smile. "What did you think I'd look like?"

Tim grinned, revealing a gap where a tooth should have been. "Thought you'd be an old battle-ax with a face to frighten the devil hisself."

Libby was intrigued. "Why should you think that?"

Tim shrugged. "Stands to reason. Can't see why no pretty woman'd want the job."

"It's an adventure," Libby said, fighting to remain calm. She didn't want either of them to learn her real reason for being there,

"Adventure!" Tim snorted. "Hell, what's a girl like you need adventure for? You should have a husband by now, couple a babies."

Libby turned to Nick Brent. "I never heard a worse male chauvinist."

Nick grinned. "Oh, he's just running off at the mouth. Truth is, though, we didn't expect anyone like you."

"I don't know why not," Libby began. "I grew up in the Texas oil fields."

"Comes the boss," said Tim softly. "And he don't look too happy. Reckon he don't like the idea of a woman in the jungle neither."

Nick's eyes grew dark. "Maybe not, though he seems to like them anywhere else."

Libby's mind registered his voice, but her eyes had gone automatically to the tall, dark man who had just entered the room. Her heart seemed to jump up in her throat and stick there, and she thrust her trembling hands into her lap to hide them. If he had been handsome before, he was even more striking now. He wore a lightweight suit that made his bronzed skin look even darker. His shoulders were just as broad, his stomach just as lean, but his face had changed. It was older, of course, more rugged. But there was more to the change than that.

Once she had thought the youthful Jared a dangerous man. But he had been only a boy compared to the powerful man who stood poised in the bar's doorway. He wore an air of insolence, wore it as arrogantly as he wore the expensively cut suit that clung to his lean frame. His gaze swept the room slowly. He was looking, no doubt, for Nick or Tim, but Libby could not be unaware of the way those arrogant, speculative eyes lingered on the faces of certain beautiful women. Nor of the responses they elicited there. She felt her own pulse quickening at the thought of those gray-green eyes boring into hers.

She twisted her hands nervously in her lap. How was Jared going to react to seeing her? He certainly had known she was coming. At least, the front office had sent her file on to him.

She dropped her eyes just before his gaze reached their table, thankful for the dim lighting that concealed the flush of her cheeks.

"He's seen us," Nick said. "Don't be afraid of him, Libby. His bark's worse than his bite."

Libby nodded. Obviously Jared had not thought fit to discuss their former status with his crew. It was probably just as well, she told herself. She did not want Nick to think of her as Mrs. Harper. Maybe once she got Jared out of her system, she and Nick . . .

She didn't need to watch Jared's approach to the table. She knew his long, sure stride, the grace and power of it. She knew, too, that other female eyes followed his progress through the room.

"Hello, Jared." Nick spoke first and his voice held only warm welcome.

"Hello, Nick. Tim."

There was a pause, and Libby's eyes left her glass to travel to Nick's friendly face. "This is Libby Collins," he said. "The newest addition to our team."

She had to look at Jared then, and slowly she raised her eyes to his. The merest flicker of emotion appeared there for an instant and then vanished.

"Good evening, Miss Collins." The emphasis on the last words was apparent only to Libby's ears.

"Good evening, Mr. Harper." She was glad her voice remained calm and steady. She could pretend as well as he could.

Jared settled himself across from her and ordered a drink. Nothing fancy for him, she noted. Just plain whiskey and soda.

Libby sipped slowly. She had never been a heavy drinker, and tonight she needed all her wits about her. She tried to concentrate on what the men were saying, tried not to look at Jared, but her eyes kept straying back to him.

Her first impression had been right. He'd grown much harder. His face looked like granite. No doubt he no longer had scruples about silly little virgins, she caught herself thinking, and knew immediate shame. That was one thing that could not be laid at Jared's door, in spite of her mother's persistent effort to do so. Libby knew quite clearly who had done the pursuing. And it had not been Jared.

A small orchestra began playing, and Nick looked at her. "How about a dance?"

Libby hesitated. This was, after all, a working trip.

"Come on," urged Nick. "Be a sport. It isn't every night I can dance with a pretty girl like you." He grinned. "Just think, you'll be saving me from all those barracudas out there just waiting to get their clutches on an innocent like me."

Tim guffawed, and Libby risked a glance at Jared, but he seemed absorbed in contemplation of his glass. "All right." The words surprised her. "Though I imagine you can protect yourself quite well," she teased as she rose and stepped into his arms.

Nick was a good dancer and, away from Jared's piercing eyes, she could relax a little. She felt quite safe in Nick's arms. "Don't worry about the boss," he whispered. "He comes on pretty strong, but basically he's a good guy." There was a moment's pause. "He—likes women—lots of them. But I don't think he'll bother you. He likes the older ones. Business exchange, so to speak. But if you need a friend, just remember I'm here."

"Thank you," Libby answered. "It's always good to have a friend. Do you suppose he really objects to taking a woman into the jungle?"

"Could be," Nick answered, dancing her further from the table. "He's got a kind of weak spot for innocence and goodness. Never takes advantage of it. And you certainly fill the bill."

Libby stifled a sigh. Jared would not think so. She felt neither good nor innocent. In spite of the fact that he was out of her sight, her body longed for Jared. If he were holding her now, she would not be relaxed; she would be trembling with pent-up desires. She simply had to get hold of herself.

When the number was over, she and Nick returned to the table. Nick was pulling out her chair to reseat her when Jared stood up. "My turn," he said and reached for her hand.

Libby felt the hard fingers close around her own, and he led her away from the table. It was useless to refuse, she told herself. What would the others think?

They reached the dance floor and Jared pulled her into his arms. She bit her bottom lip in an effort to contain the small sound of pleasure that rose in her throat.

"You dance very well," Jared observed.

"So do you," she replied, calling to memory the nights she had begged him to take her dancing and he had refused, claiming he didn't know how. "You must have had a good teacher." She hoped he didn't hear the cattiness in her tone.

"Arthur Murray," he said coldly. "Women like to dance. So I've been told."

"Yes, they do," Libby answered, trying to match his coldness. "Especially with their husbands."

The arm that encircled her waist drew her closer until she could feel her breasts touching his chest. He laughed harshly. "I'm afraid I know nothing of that," he said. "My one excursion into matrimony was more than sufficient to sour me on the whole idea."

Inexorably his arm drew her closer still. She felt the long, lean length of his thighs against hers. The heat of his body, the clean, male smell of him seemed to envelope her in an aura of desire. It was useless to tell herself that he had lied to her, cheated on her, probably never loved her at all. At this moment, with his body so close to hers, none of that mattered. She wanted him. She wanted him so badly that it was all she could do to keep from pressing herself even more tightly against him, from rising on tiptoe to touch his mouth with hers. Surely he hadn't forgotten how good it had been for them. How could anyone forget that? She fought the desire to lay her head against his shoulder.

His speaking startled her so that she jumped, her body coming even nearer to his. "What are you doing here?" he asked. The question was all too clearly an accusation.

"I should think that's obvious," she replied. "I'm doing my job."

He shook his head, his cheek brushing hers momentarily and making her quiver with longing. "The jungle's no place for a woman. Not a woman like you."

"I'll take care of my career," she said crisply. "And you can take care of yours."

She heard the hiss of his indrawn breath and waited for the explosion of his anger. But it did not come. He had matured. He knew how to control his anger now.

He said no more to her, but his arm tightened and tightened until her breasts were crushed against his jacket, until she thought she would suffocate with her need for him. His hard thighs moved against hers at every step they took, and gradually Libby realized that there was something that the years had not changed. No matter what he might say, Jared's body was responding to hers. He might be trying to humiliate her by making her understand that she still wanted him. But that, she told herself, was a two-way street. She might want Jared, as indeed she did, in spite of her knowledge of his character. But that wanting was not one-sided. Jared's need was just as strong. And she had no intention of meeting it, she told herself severely. But the surge of elation that swept over her would not be denied.

He did not ask her to dance again, nor did Nick. They took their drinks into Hin's Heavenly Cookhouse and dined on something delicious that Libby promptly forgot the name of. She was not really conscious of anything else around her; Jared's presence was so physically overwhelming. She ate because it was expected of her. And she nursed the one drink through the entire evening, frightened of combining much alcohol with the emotions rioting through her.

They did not linger long after dinner. As they finished dessert, Jared spoke. "We're making an early start in the morning. Better get plenty of sleep." His statement seemed to be addressed to all three of them, but his eyes stayed longest on Libby's face. She nodded with the others.

Jared pushed back his chair. "Got a couple last-minute things to attend to. I'm sure you'll see Libby to her room, Nick."

Libby felt there was something vaguely insulting in this last statement, and she hurried to say, "That's not necessary."

Jared's eyes were hard. "As you wish," he replied. "Just remember this is a dangerous town for a woman alone."

He was on his feet and gone before the full import of his words reached her. Then she swallowed an exclamation of indignation. He sounded as though she meant to look for someone to spend the night with!

Frowning, Tim shook his head. "Hope he ain't gonna be so tetchy through the whole trip. Something's sure bugging him."

Nick's smile was a little nervous. "He'll get over it, whatever it is. We know it hasn't anything to do with us. You ready?"

Libby nodded. "Yes, I am kind of beat. Good night, Tim."

"Night."

Nick's fingers were light on her elbow as he guided her toward the elevator.

"The bill," Libby began.

"The boss'll sign the tab."

Libby sighed. Jared was her boss, too, and it was not something she liked to think about. She knew her job well, but she was not used to working in the wet and steamy jungle. The heat she had felt outside would be even worse in the middle of the rain forest.

Nick paused outside her door. "Sleep well," he said. "I'll call you for wake-up." His glance lingered on her long, blond hair lying free on her shoulders. "Got a jungle hat?"

Libby shook her head. "No, I meant to get one here."

"No problem," Nick said. "I have an extra. You did bring your own boots?"

Libby grinned. "Of course. And standard jungle gear. Don't worry, Nick. I don't intend to go out there like this."

His expression lightened. "It's a darn good thing," he replied, his eyes sliding over her figure, molded by the softly flowing dress.

"I appreciate your concern, Nick. Really. But I am a qualified geologist. Not a dumb blonde. And as for this"—she pulled at a strand of hair—"I always wear it braided up in the field. It simplifies matters."

Nick's smile became sheepish. "Sorry," he said. "Just trying to help. You were really a surprise to all of us."

Not to Jared, she told herself silently. He knew I was coming, and he was prepared for me. "Good night, Nick. And thank you."

"Good night, Libby."

She closed and locked the door and began immediately to get ready for bed. It took a matter of moments to lay out her clothes for the next day, to separate her few dresses and pantsuits from her working clothes. Then she shook out the thin cotton nightshirt she had chosen both for its coolness and its light weight.

The bed looked inviting, and Libby showered again and climbed gratefully between the cool sheets. It would probably be some time before she slept in such comfort again.

But, tired as she was, she couldn't relax and sleep.

Every time she closed her eyes, she saw Jared's dark, accusing face, the hard lines etched around his mouth, the strong jut of his jaw. Even with her eyes open she could feel the length of his body against hers, inflaming it.

"Damn," said Libby to the empty room. Why did I ever meet him? And why did I chase him like that? She turned restlessly in the bed. He's cruel and hard, she reminded herself. And I'm going to get over him. I am. I'm not going to let that man ruin the rest of my life.

3

~~~~~~~~~~~~~~~~

It was several hours later when Libby, who had finally managed to doze off, came awake to an insistent knocking on her door. Acting more on reflex than on anything else, she threw back the covers and stumbled to the door, opening it a crack.

"Jared! What do you want?" Dimly her mind registered that he was in his shirt sleeves and that he had changed his boots for sandals. His face was expressionless. "Let me in, Libby. I have to talk to you. About the job."

"I . . . can't we wait till morning?" She was not going to let him bully her.

"No!" Before she could say anything else he had pushed his way into the room and shut the door.

Libby retreated slightly. "You—you've no right in here," she said. "This is *my* room."

"I have things to say to you." His eyes raked over her, settling on her breasts, plainly visible beneath the thin cotton material.

Libby felt a flush rising to her cheeks. She turned to look for her robe; she must cover herself. She moved toward her suitcase, but he was there, his hands grasping her bare upper arms. A wave of desire shot through her, weakening her, but she kept her voice even. "What is it you want?"

"Libby, do you know what you're doing? This isn't Texas we're going into. It's jungle, tropical rain forest. It's hot, with humidity like you've never experienced before."

"I can handle it," she said, willing herself to stand quietly, not to heed the racing of her blood, the pounding of her heart that his nearness caused.

"No, you can't." His voice grew harsher. "It's not just the heat and the humidity. The jungle is full of death, Libby. Rotting animals, rotting plants; it's a kind of world you can't even imagine."

"Then it's time I experienced it." She fought to keep her head clear. She could not give in to the desire that was enveloping her.

"Don't be so silly," he said softly, his eyes warming as he gazed down at her. "There are bugs in the jungle, Libby, all kinds of them. They get inside your clothes. In your hair. In your food."

"I can handle it," she repeated, not acknowledging, even to herself, how his words frightened her.

"Libby, listen to me." He shook her lightly as though to get her attention. "You've got to give this up. Go back to the States."

She shook her head. "No, Jared. I won't. This is my job. If I go back now, it'll look really bad for me. You know that. I don't want a blot on my record."

"You've got to go back," he insisted, almost as though he hadn't heard anything she'd said. "I'll arrange it in the morning."

"Jared!" Her voice rose sharply. "I'm not leaving. Get that through your head. This is my *job*. And I'm going to do it."

"Libby, please. This is for your own good. I'm concerned for you."

She stared at him in astonishment. Concerned! Now she was really angry. How could he expect her to believe a thing like that? But before she could make a sharp retort, he gave a strangled moan and pulled her into his arms. Automatically she fought him. So many of their quarrels had ended like this. The issue not resolved but pushed aside and forgotten, at least momentarily, while he kissed her into submission. But then there had been love—or at least the semblance of it—between them. Now she was not sure she could put a name to this fever racing through her, unless it was pure physical desire.

His lips sought hers, and Libby twisted in his arms, conscious that only the flimsy nightshirt covered her nakedness. But her twisting only caused it to ride up, and she felt the coolness of his belt buckle against her naked stomach. "Jared! No! Let me go! You—must—let me—go!"

His hand found her bare thigh and stroked it gently,

and all the long years without him seemed to be gathered into one great fever of desire. It had always been like this, she thought. With the merest caress he had been able to kindle desire in her. But not now. Now she would withstand him. She didn't intend to be used in this way.

"Jared! No! Have you no decency?" She forced the words out.

His laugh grated on her already highly strung nerves. "Not where you're concerned," he growled. His eyes bored into hers. First they were hot, then they went suddenly cold. "No, making love to you won't solve anything," he said.

Libby could not think of a reply.

"I didn't have this in mind," he continued, "when I came up here. I just wanted to talk to you. To make you understand that you can't stay. But when I saw you, in that next-to-nothing nightshirt—"

Still she was speechless.

"I still think you should go back to the States."

"No." She made the word as firm as she could. "Jared, you must understand. I can't do that."

His eyes grew even harder; and bitter lines were etched deep in his face. "You'd better be careful," he said gruffly. "Out there in the jungle men lose their civilized veneer."

Libby's laugh was harsh. "I suppose you call *that kiss* civilized."

"You liked it," he said harshly. "I know that much."

"You're despicable." Libby cried. "You've grown even worse than you used to be."

His laughter grated on her ears. "You haven't seen anything yet. Better run while you can."

"No." His eyes had fallen to her breasts, and belatedly she crossed her arms over them.

"Go back to sleep," he said gruffly. "If you're still fool enough to go along, you'll need your rest." His eyes turned tender. "Please, Libby. Let me get you a flight home."

"No, no, *no*." She was getting close to screaming now. She could feel it. The trip had been long and tiring, and her argument with Jared had left her almost exhausted. She wanted to fall back on the bed and cry—cry in great gasping sobs. But first she had to get him out of the room.

"Good night, Jared." She raised her eyes to his. For a moment she glimpsed the kindling of desire deep in their depths, then he shook himself, like a dog ridding itself of wetness, and turned toward the door. "Think about what I said," he stated and let himself out.

For long moments Libby stared at the door, then she jumped up and rushed to lock it. That done, she moved slowly back toward the rumpled bed.

With a groan of despair she threw herself onto it and buried her face in the pillow. Nothing was working out right. This trip was supposed to kill her feelings for Jared, and instead they were only growing stronger.

4

Morning found Libby heavy-eyed and listless. She had cried for some time, literally cried herself to sleep, but she had wakened only an hour later, and sleep had returned slowly. Nick's wake-up call roused her from what was actually her first restful slumber of the night, but she wasted no time bemoaning the fact.

It was clear that Jared didn't want her along, but it seemed equally clear that he couldn't send her home without a legitimate reason. After all, the company had quite strict guidelines about avoiding discrimination against female employees. He would have to prove her incompetent in order to get rid of her. And she meant to give him no opportunity.

She was down in the lobby, her waterproof case in hand, well before the appointed time. Fortunately Tim and Nick arrived before Jared, so she didn't have to face him alone.

Nick eyed her critically. "Better nap on the plane," he said. "You still look beat."

Libby managed a bright smile. "Nonsense, I'm raring to go."

She was spared Nick's somewhat skeptical reply as Tim hefted his pack. "Here comes the boss."

Shouldering her pack before one of the men could reach for it, Libby stood waiting as Jared crossed the lobby. He looked none the worse for their argument last night, she thought grimly. But then he'd always moved with assured grace. Even when he'd returned from the fields close to exhaustion.

"All ready?" Jared inquired. He looked just as striking in his working khakis as he had in last night's suit. Libby could feel her body responding to all that masculinity.

"All ready," answered the men, and Libby echoed them.

"Good. The car's waiting." And he led the way to the entrance, not even condescending to give her a glance.

Trailing along behind the others, Libby didn't know whether to feel relief or anger. Finally she smiled at herself. She probably ought to be pleased. If he'd pinned her with those piercing eyes of his, he might have read the desire in hers.

To her shame, she couldn't erase her desire for him. Remembrance of his kisses coursed through her now, making her throb with longing for his touch. But he wouldn't have her again, she told herself with determination.

She settled into the back seat of the car, determined to forget the turmoil in her mind, determined to enjoy the sights of the exotic city they were moving through. The taxi crept by necessity, because of the multitude of people. Libby craned her neck, trying to see the tops of great blocks of apartment buildings, clean clothes fluttering from flagpoles on their balconies. She admired the bold, Chinese-lettered banners that served some establishments as signs. She only wished she could read what they said.

The crowd on the streets showed more diversity than that at the airport. Here there were cheongsams and saris, but there were also sarongs and turbans, and young people in blue jeans and cowboy boots cruising along on motorcycles.

"It's a fascinating city," observed Nick. "When we get back, I'll show you some of it."

"Thank you," Libby replied, managing a smile, though she had noticed a tightening of Jared's jaw. "I'd like that."

The drive to the airport didn't take long. The car deposited them beside a sleek little Lear jet. It was still quite early and the heat was not yet bad. Libby turned to Nick. "The company takes care of us, all right."

He gave her a swift smile but did not reply. She climbed out of the car before either of the men could get around to help her. She didn't want any favors;

she intended to carry her own weight on this trip, and she might as well start now. Grasping her pack, she set out after the others as they boarded the little plane.

Libby knew the value of the neat little jet. Of course, she should have expected something like it. Theirs was an experienced crew. Even she herself was valuable to the company. And there were vast stretches of water out here. It was one thing to fly a puddle jumper over dry country, where there was room to land safely if difficulties developed, and quite another to crash-land in the South China Sea.

She stowed her pack with the others and settled into her seat, automatically fastening the seat belt around her waist. The seat beside her was empty. Tim and Nick were in the seat ahead of her; their whispered discussion did not quite reach her ears. Jared sat further up with the pilot. She closed her eyes and leaned back in the seat. She had to do some serious thinking.

There was still time to back out of this. In spite of her words to Jared she was fairly confident that she could get the front office to accept an excuse for leaving. But the question was, did she want to? Certainly her plan to get Jared out of her system wasn't working so far. From the first moment she saw him, standing there in the doorway of the bar like he owned the place, she had been even more in his power. And last night—last night his kisses had reinforced that power.

Instead of fading from her life, he was gaining even more prominence in it. But should she turn tail and run from him? That was clearly what he wanted. She would not, however. She knew this with sudden

47

certainty. There was no need to manufacture fancy excuses for the front office because she didn't intend to return till this assignment was over. She meant to stick it out to the bitter end—whatever that might be.

If only she had stuck it out years ago, she thought. If only she hadn't been so young and immature. They had been so happy, so much in love. With their whole lives before them. And she had let it all escape her. What if she'd worked as hard at making their marriage go as she had at getting Jared to run off with her? Could they have made it then?

But, no, she'd had to listen to her mother. Had to let the little hints, the little seeds of doubt, sprout in her suspicious mind. What if Jared *had* turned to someone else? She'd forced him to it. *If* he really had. She was no longer even sure of that. The one thing she *was* sure of was that she'd been a child. A spoiled-rotten child masquerading in a woman's body. She'd been selfish and nasty, thinking only of her own needs. No wonder he had found it impossible to live with her.

She sighed. Why did learning have to be such a difficult process? And why did people always seem to learn things when it was too late to do any good? Like now. Now she could see clearly that she had been much at fault. At least half the blame had been hers. Maybe more.

She should never have listened to her mother. Why hadn't she been more supicious of her mother's sudden interest in her affairs? She'd never liked Jared; she'd always called him "that roustabout" in a tone that made the words an insult. She'd never taken a great deal of interest in Libby's life before that either, except to try to get her interested in young men from the best families.

But suddenly there were phone calls every day, invitations to shopping trips. Bored and lonely, Libby had welcomed her mother's company. And it had been fun sprucing up the little house, until Jared started to complain about the money she was spending—money that belonged to her parents.

Stupid and selfish she had called him then, but the truth was that those words applied more to her. Of course Jared didn't want her to use her parents' money. Fiercely independent, he had been on his own since he was thirteen. And if he hadn't much to show for it, he had told her once angrily, it was because before her he'd had nothing to work for. Now that he had a wife things were going to be different.

And he had worked, worked himself practically to exhaustion, she thought, flushing with shame. He shouldn't have had to work like that for a petulant, spoiled girl who never gave him a moment's rest.

Tears prickled under her closed eyelids. Leaving Jared had been a big mistake, the biggest mistake in her life. But right now there didn't seem to be much chance to remedy it. He was determined to see her as the spoiled child she had once been. This trip was her only chance to convince him otherwise. And she was going to give it her best shot, she thought as sleep finally overtook her.

The Lear jet touched down like a floating feather, so lightly it didn't even disturb Libby's sleep. It was Jared's hand on her shoulder that shook her awake.

49

"Time to get moving," he said, and his eyes told her plainly that she had already been branded a weakling.

She struggled erect in the seat. "Okay, boss," she replied, keeping her voice completely without nuance.

For a moment his hand slid slowly toward her throat, then with the merest touch of a caress on her cheek he turned away. She felt the rush of blood to her face. That caress had been a warning. She knew it. He knew her weaknesses, it seemed to say. And he would use them.

She bent to unbuckle her seat belt. Fussing with it would give the telltale blush time to fade. It was important to keep the others from knowing that something was wrong between her and Jared. A survey crew had to work together, especially in dangerous situations. It was important that they respect each other. Undercurrents of fear and anger would only destroy their confidence. In a crucial moment that might even cost them their lives.

Libby shouldered her pack and followed the others outside. The air was warmer now, hot—and heavy with moisture. Breathing seemed to take concentrated effort. But she accepted this calmly. She would get used to it. She would get used to anything this trip threw at her. For she was absolutely determined to stick it out, to prove to Jared Harper that she was no longer the selfish, ignorant child who had once been his wife.

With this in mind she wasted no time in looking around her. This was all old stuff to Jared and the others. She didn't intend to stand around gawking like a tourist. So when he reached the car that waited for them, she was right there behind him. His eyes revealed a little flicker of surprise as he turned and saw her waiting there. But he said nothing, and it was Nick who opened the back door and motioned her inside.

As she settled herself on the seat, she knew that her khakis were already wet. What a humid country, she thought, wiping absently at her upper lip where beads of perspiration were forming. From what Jared had said, it was full of unpleasant animal and insect life, too. Even the air seemed designed to make one uncomfortable.

As the car moved forward and the air conditioning began to work, she stifled a sigh. Evidently she didn't stifle it completely, for Nick gave her a sympathetic smile. She returned it briefly, then turned her attention to the window. Some distance away she could see a cluster of modern-looking buildings. "What's over there?" she asked as the car bumped along the rough roadbed. So this was Balikpapan.

"A lot of the chippies and oilies live there," Nick explained. "It's close to the beach. All prefab, air-conditioned stuff."

"Oilies?" Libby began.

From the front seat Tim guffawed. "Oilies work for the oil company," he explained. "Chippies are lumbermen. A lot of Americans, Europeans and Australians stay in these camps."

The drive to town was short. Jared stopped the car by a warehouselike building. "You and Nick get things in order," he said. "And get some lunch. I'm going to give Libby a look at the town. We'll be back in a couple hours."

Though she didn't look at Nick, Libby heard the

quick intake of his breath. Tim, however, seemed to find this perfectly acceptable. "Okay, boss."

"You might as well come up here," Jared said to her as Tim climbed out. "That way I won't have to yell."

Libby wasted no time in vain protests. Whatever Jared's reasons for this peculiar sightseeing trip, she wasn't going to let him throw her. She waved goodbye to Nick and Tim as she settled into the front seat. Until Jared chose to make this into something else, she was going to regard the drive as a tourist excursion.

"If you're hungry, we can have lunch first. You'll like the Total Beach House. Union Oil runs it."

"Does it serve native food?" Libby asked.

Jared shrugged. "You want native food you go to the natives."

"I'd like to taste some native dishes," Libby said. "I think that's a way of broadening my appreciation of other cultures." She wondered if he was thinking of one of their early arguments, rare in that it didn't concern money or time. He had wanted her to try some Mexican chili at a little place he knew, and she had protested that she didn't like hot, spicy food. He'd given in, she remembered. She remembered, too, that after that he'd never suggested a Mexican restaurant again.

For a moment Jared was silent, and Libby concentrated on the passing scenery. Then he spoke. "I could take you to the Atomic. They've got delicious chili crayfish."

"That sounds like fun," Libby said, hiding her small smile of triumph. His tone had been carefully controlled, and she had not dared risk a glance at his face, but the mention of chili convinced her that Jared remembered. She would be willing to eat anything, no matter how spicy and hot, to convince Jared that she had grown up.

"Okay. But first I want to take you up to Pasir Ridge."

Libby managed to look at him calmly. "What's that?"

Jared's smile was rather bitter. "Most of your compatriots don't have such a tolerance for native culture." His tone indicated that he believed her own tolerance was affected. "When they come over here, they expect to have all the amenities of home. Or more. Pasir Ridge—Kampung Amerika, as the natives call it—was built for them. It has everything. Swimming pools, smooth roads, neat little rows of houses, nice green lawns. Suburbia transported intact."

The scorn was evident in his voice. "They even have movies and Sunday night bingo. Most wives never leave the place."

He swerved the car expertly to avoid the big pothole in the road. They were leaving the native part of town behind them, and Libby gasped as they entered the foreign district. It was unbelievable how the surroundings had changed. Everything Jared had said was true. The neat little houses sat in row after row, their paved driveways and smooth green lawns like any in the States.

Jared continued to drive until he reached a place where he could park the car. "Get out," he said, and she followed him obediently to the side of the road.

"You can see it all from here."

She looked out. The neat houses with their patchlike lawns made a colorful picture. Out in the harbor she could see oil rigs and the big tankers that would carry their product. She brought her gaze back to Kampung Amerika and then further down the hillside where the scene changed dramatically, where the cleanliness of suburbia gave way to dirt and chaos, to sprawling hovels and, in the far distance, to white-washed huts.

Libby suppressed another shiver as she gazed out. "I don't know which is worse," she whispered, more to herself than to Jared. "The poverty and filth or the civilization that disregards it."

Jared made no reply to this, but as she had expected none, she was not immediately aware that he was looking at her. When she grew conscious of his regard, she turned slowly to meet it.

"I suppose neither of them is exactly commend-able," he said then. "This is a country of paradoxes. You'll see lots of Sumatran young people in Western clothes. Big, shiny American cars on these abominable roads. Over there," he gestured. "There's a nightclub hanging on a hill over a simple fishing village. Some-times villagers wear Western clothes. Sometimes they wear native. And sometimes they wear a mixture of both."

Libby nodded. "The land itself is paradoxical," she said. "There's so much beauty and so much ugli-ness."

Looking at Jared like this, standing close to him, made it difficult to concentrate. All morning his pres-ence had been pulling on her consciousness. Right this minute she could feel her breath quickening. She wanted to be swept into his arms, to feel his lean, hard body against her own.

Without thinking, she raised her eyes to his. They were not cool now, those gray-green eyes that could glitter like ice. Warmth shone from them. For a moment Libby felt that he was going to kiss her. She could see the desire in his gaze. But then the moment was gone. He dropped his eyes and turned back toward the lower reaches of town.

Libby bit back a sigh. It was good that he hadn't touched her, she told herself sternly. She would never be able to escape his influence if he kept kissing her, if he held her as he had last night. Heat sped over her body, and she knew that this heat had nothing to do with climate. She wanted Jared. She wanted to be in his arms, to feel his caresses, to belong to him as fully and completely as possible.

Sudden tears pricked at her eyes. She had belonged to him once, more completely and fully than she had ever imagined possible. But in her youthful ignorance she had lost it. She swallowed hastily and blinked back the tears. If only she could talk to him, tell him she was sorry. But last night he had been so hard, so unyielding. He couldn't see past the spoiled girl she'd been to the woman she'd become. And she wanted him to. She wanted it very much. At least he could recognize that she had changed, had grown.

Climbing into the car again, she cast him a furtive glance. She wanted to know what he had done in those missing years besides knocking about the world. But she dared not ask him anything so personal. Dared not do anything that might disturb the rather uneasy truce existing between them.

They got into the car and Jared turned back toward the town. Libby kept her eyes on the scene around her. The silence between them lengthened. Finally, more to ease it than to gain information, she spoke. "Can you tell me something about the job?"

"It's a routine survey trip," he replied, and she noted with relief that his voice carried no sarcasm. "We've already done a lot of work on the area. We've made several flights over it. Used the magnetometer. The results were promising."

Libby nodded. "So the rock formations look right."

Jared smiled, but without humor. "There's a lot of oil in this country, Libby. But it's no easier to find than back home. Sinking a well outside the lowest closing contour will get you a dry hole every time, certainly. But sinking one within it is no guarantee of getting a paying one."

"Of course." She was not insulted by his words. He was offering information. "And the seismograph?"

He shook his head. "The jungle's too thick to haul that stuff all the way through it. That's going to be our job. We'll get the feel of the land. Look for the best places for crews to test. The government owns all the oil here." He smiled dryly. "Nobody gets rich quick on it. At least not legally. They probably won't want to drill right away, but they want some idea of what they may have. And the best places to look later. So that's what we're going to give them."

"I see." Libby's voice was calm. There had been a covert reference there to her own father. It was no secret in the Texas fields that Sam Collins was a bad man to cross. Several of his biggest deals were widely thought to have been underhanded and the next thing to illegal, but nevertheless Sam had prospered. And so, as his daughter, had she.

She wanted to tell Jared that she'd been no part of that, that she couldn't be blamed for Sam's sins. That she no longer even benefited from them. But fear held her back. And besides, would Jared even believe her?

As they left Kampung Amerika the smooth, tarred road became a mass of potholes, and Jared gave more of his attention to his driving. He was a good driver, swift but careful, and she observed that his reflexes were as quick as ever. Her memory took her back to the past; to those first trips to the movies in his battered old car.

"Why did you decide on geology?" Jared asked suddenly. "Especially the looking-for-oil kind."

Libby tried to keep her feelings from showing. "I've always loved the oil business. The fields, the excitement. It's in my blood." She wished she hadn't said that when she saw the way his jaw tightened. She was Sam's daughter. There was no way to beat that.

"So you decided to become a rockhound."

Libby smiled at the expression. "Right. Or more correctly," she added, not wanting him to think her conceited, "I'm probably still a pebble pup."

Jared shook his head. "I suppose that you have a diploma. *And* some experience. That makes you a legitimate rockhound." For the first time since her arrival, he gave her a genuine smile. Libby basked in its warmth.

"How did you make the move from roughneck to—" She paused, uncertain of his status.

"Actually, I'm a geophysicist," he said dryly. "I got sort of tired of being a roustabout."

"But you were a roughneck when—" She couldn't go on.

"And a driller after that," he said, ignoring her pause. "Once I got bitten by the bug of ambition I couldn't stop."

Libby knew the hours of hard work and experience that a man had to have before he could become a roughneck, or assistant to the driller. Roustabouts were just common laborers; they only needed strong arms. But roughnecks, and the drillers they aspired to replace, had to know their business—and know it well.

"Finally I decided to use my brains to find the stuff, rather than to keep things running smoothly. So I took myself off to school. South Dakota School of Mines. And you?"

"Colorado," she answered automatically. No wonder Jared had made such a name for himself. He knew more about the oil business than most. He could find possible oil-bearing sites and at the same time consider the more practical problems of drilling. "Actually, a lot of my training was in photogeology," she continued. "But I don't know how useful that will be when we're dealing with the jungle. I can also evaluate rock strata and sand. Things like that." She felt suddenly defensive.

"Your training seems adequate," Jared said. "The company always sends out a dossier on newcomers."

"If you knew that," Libby said, forgetting her resolve to be cautious, "why did you think I couldn't do the job?"

"You're a woman." He used the word almost as an insult. "I'm not saying you don't have the brains. You just don't have the stamina for this kind of thing.

Tigers, rhinoceroses, orangutans. Those are just a few of the animals we're apt to meet out there. To say nothing of snakes and all kinds of insects. It's just no place for a woman. If I'd had my way, they'd have sent the photos back to the States for you to study. You shouldn't be out here at all."

Libby decided to ignore that. "What happened to the man I was sent out to replace?"

"Murphy?"

"Yes."

"He contracted some sort of jungle fever. Had to be hospitalized. Which just goes to prove my point." He gave her a hard glance.

"I don't see why." Libby didn't want to pick a quarrel, but she had to stick up for herself. "Murphy's a man."

Jared swerved, neatly missing another pothole, and smiled condescendingly. "If a man can't take this country, how can a woman?" he asked.

Unconsciously Libby straightened her shoulders. "You're being unfair. I'm as healthy as any man. And you know it. I've had all my inoculations. I'm not going to get sick."

Jared shook his head. "As usual, you don't have all the facts. There are fevers in these jungles that no one has even named, let alone found a way to inoculate against." He shook his head, a frown puckering his forehead. "It's a bad place, Libby. I don't like the idea of your going there."

"I have to," she said simply. "It's my job." She did not reply to the tacit accusation in the words "as usual." It was true that she had been prone to jump to conclusions during their time together. But everything had seemed to conspire against them then, including their own immaturity.

By this time Jared was pulling up to the restaurant. "Time for that chili crayfish," he said, and she could not help hearing the anticipation in his voice.

5

That evening Libby sat across a table from the three men. They had reached Samarinda in good time and were having dinner before retiring for a good night's rest. They would be making an early start in the morning.

Absently Libby stirred her drink. Lunch had been a huge success, at least from her point of view. She had truly enjoyed the glimpses of Balikpapan that Jared had allowed her, and the chili crayfish had been excellent. Jared could not know, of course, that she had developed a taste for highly spiced food, including the Mexican chili she had once refused to try with him, and he had seemed rather quiet afterward. But she didn't intend to worry about that.

"So everything's in shape," Jared was saying, and her eyes went automatically to his face.

She loved the look of it. His skin was darkened by the sun, as it had always been, and the laugh lines around his eyes were etched deeper than she remembered. Once she had known every line and contour of that beloved face, had known his body, too, the long, lean length of it, under her hands, pressing against her own.

She felt desire beginning to rise and quickly wrenched her eyes away. One thing she was determined about. Jared might never love her again, but by the time this trip was over, he would recognize that she had changed. The spoiled brat had become a woman.

"What'll it be tonight, Tim?" Libby's attention was called back to the present by Jared's deep voice. "Roasted crocodile or turtle?"

Libby swallowed hastily and tried to keep her expression even. Crocodile? She didn't glance at Jared, but she felt sure that he was putting on a show for her benefit.

"Guess I'll have crocodile," said Tim with evident relish. "Tickles me to eat one of them old devils as is always hoping to get a man."

Libby's hands, out of sight under the table, clenched into fists. She couldn't eat crocodile. She just couldn't.

"What about you, Nick?"

Nick's glance moved around the table, pausing for the merest moment on Libby's pale face. "I've been waiting for some *udang golah.* I've always been fond of shrimp, and the giant river ones are really great the way they fry them here."

Jared nodded. Then came the moment she'd been dreading. "And you, Libby?"

"I think I'll have the shrimp, too." She tried to make her voice firm.

The glimmer of amusement in Jared's eyes was quite clear, and she forced herself not to rise to the bait. It was stupid of him to think that because she didn't want to eat crocodile or turtle she couldn't pull her weight on the team. Or maybe this was subtle revenge for the surprise she had dealt him at lunch time.

The shrimp were delicious, and she managed the rest of her dinner with aplomb. Then Nick turned to her. "You're sure you have everything you need in the way of clothes?"

"I'm sure, Nick. I'll be fine."

Jared smiled, a grim smile that she didn't like at all. "It's wise to have suitable clothes, of course. But where the leeches are concerned it doesn't matter. They'll get inside the best-laced boots. Inside your pants, your shirt." He grimaced. "Little devils can get anywhere."

Libby controlled a shiver and remained silent. He was remembering her aversion to spiders, she thought. And he was trying to scare her off. But it wouldn't work. She wouldn't let it.

"The best thing to do," said Jared with a smug smile, "is to go native. If you aren't wearing any clothes, they've no place to hide."

His eyes met hers then, and she knew suddenly that he was mentally undressing her. She felt the scarlet flood her cheeks and saw his lips curl in amusement. Then his eyes grew even warmer, so warm that before she was aware of it her tongue had flicked out to lick her upper lip. She read triumph in his eyes then. He knew how to excite her, and he was going to take every opportunity to make her uncomfortable and frustrated. But she was going to handle it, she told herself again.

"Do you smoke?" Nick asked.

Startled, Libby shook her head. "No."

"Too bad. Applying the tip of a lighted cigarette makes the little devils let go."

"Can't you just pull them off?" she asked, carefully avoiding Jared's eyes.

"No! If you do that, you leave the suction apparatus in your skin. Then infection may set in."

This time Libby could not quite contain her shudder.

"Ah, they ain't nothing," said Tim as he leaned back precariously in his chair. "You get used to 'em after a while. And their bites don't hurt none." He grinned. "Rather face leeches than crocs any day."

The wave of revulsion seemed to start at the base of Libby's belly and rise upward toward her throat. Under cover of the table she dug her nails into her palms. The pain helped to clear her head, helped to keep her nausea under control.

Nick's eyes met hers briefly, and his smile was sheepish. "I think we've teased the greenhorn long enough. The leeches are there, Libby, but we've got good repellent. They don't bother us much."

"Ain't no repellent for crocs and rhinos and such," volunteered Tim, his eyes sparkling with glee.

Libby turned toward him. "I wouldn't want to venture out in the jungle at all if I were you," she said.

Tim bit. "An' why not?"

Libby's tone was serious. "Who knows how many relatives your dinner had? Why, half the crocs in the jungle could be after you. I imagine they're laying their plans right now."

For just a moment Tim took her words at face value. Then he broke into great guffaws of laughter.

Libby's smile was devilish. "I wouldn't laugh if I were you, Tim. Maybe the crocs have their own jungle grapevine. And it's saying, 'Get Tim.'"

"Nah." He gave her a sly look. "Besides, even if they did, the little demon didn't know whose plate he was going to end up on in time to let anyone know." And, greatly satisfied by his own wit, Tim hitched his chair even further backward. It teetered there for a moment before it went crashing down, and Tim with it. His grin, as he picked himself up off the floor, was subdued.

"I think it's time we went to bed," Jared commented, getting to his feet. "There's a jungle out there waiting for us tomorrow."

As usual, it was Nick who walked to her room with her, who arranged for her wake-up call. Libby went obediently to bed. She knew she would need all her rest. But once between the sheets it was impossible to sleep. She kept thinking of Jared, of their day together and of the way he had looked at her over the table.

Every footstep in the hall set her to trembling, her body twisting on the hard bed. She wanted him. She wanted him with every fiber in her being.

Angrily she stared at the whitewashed ceiling. She

had to get over this. She wouldn't be able to carry her weight in the jungle if she couldn't sleep properly. She made herself relax and finally sleep came.

Midafternoon of the next day found them well up the river. The *longbots,* narrow canoes equipped with outboard motors, moved easily through the muddy water, steered by the native guides Jared had hired.

At first she had wondered if he intended her to be frightened by these ferocious-looking natives with their heavily tattooed bodies clad only in the strip of brightly colored cloth called a *kain.* But she had found Kustarto and Njo interesting rather than fearsome. In fact, she soon had Njo telling her all about life in his long house.

"You like *lamin,*" he said as he guided the *longbot* skillfully past a floating log. "Much good there."

Libby smiled. She could relax for a while. Jared was in the other canoe with Nick. Tim, who shared this one with her and Njo, was dozing peacefully.

"What do you mean?"

Njo's brown forehead crinkled in a frown as his deep-brown eyes scanned the river. "Good feeling," he said finally. "Hard to tell. Little ones to see grow. Others to sit and talk. Woman cooking. Dogs, pigs, chickens. Under house." He nodded sagely. "Good there."

"What is the house like?" asked Libby, idly watching the broad banks of the river as the canoe moved slowly upstream.

"House long," said Njo. "Built on legs. Off dirt. No water if river come up. Chickens, pigs, dogs. Live under house."

"Why do they call it a long house?"

Njo's face split into a wide grin, revealing startlingly black teeth.

"*Lamin* much long," he explained. "Many, many families. Much doors."

Libby tried to visualize this. "If it's built up high, how do you get in and out?"

"Log with steps cut," Njo said. "Pull up at night. No snakes, no tigers. All safe. Enemies keep out."

"Do you have enemies now?" Libby asked.

Njo shook his head. "That old time. Dayak great headhunters. Take many heads. My grandfather tell me. Heads have much magic. Make rain. Save from sickness. Make rice grow. Heads much good." He grinned slyly. "Give to woman. Make her like Njo. Make him big man in village."

Libby swallowed an urge to laugh. What would she have done if Jared had come courting, carrying a dried head? It was certainly a different approach than candy and flowers, she thought; but in Njo's culture it was equally effective.

"How could a head do all that?" The question was not really directed at the guide, but he answered it. "Hunter take head of great warrior. Spirit live in head. Have much magic." Njo's eyes took on a faraway look. "Grandfather say old days best. Many heads hang on veranda. Village have much rice. No sickness. No fighting."

Libby nodded. "It sounds like a pleasant life."

Njo smiled. "Life in my village good. No loud noise, no too many people. Grandfather right, I think, old ways best." The motor coughed once and his attention swung to it. When he looked back to Libby, he was frowning again. "But motor new way. Make easy go up river."

"What's it like up river?" she asked.

"Like this some way." Njo waved a brown hand. "Logs in water. River big. Get smaller more we go. Up river *ulo*. Not known. Only traders go. River gets smaller. Trees come out. Not good."

"Do you think we'll stop at any *kampungs?*" The guide's picture of idyllic native life appealed to her in spite of his talk of dried heads.

"Maybe so. Njo no know. Boss say when."

Another question trembled on Libby's tongue, a question about that boss, but she swallowed it. She couldn't ask questions about Jared. How the guides reacted to him was already apparent.

Njo nodded again, eyes gleaming with mischief, and announced, "Boss big warrior. Good to take his head."

A picture of Jared's severed head, dried and dangling from a pole, presented itself to Libby with such startling clarity that she had to swallow hard to control her nausea. But, aware that Njo was watching her, she laughed at his little joke. "Yes," she agreed. "I suppose it would have been."

Njo laughed. "Take big man to get boss head. Njo no like try."

"Have you a woman?" Libby asked, trying to avoid this rather unsettling subject.

Njo nodded. "Yes. Very pretty. Nice black teeth. Ears much long."

Libby frowned. "Black teeth?"

Njo smiled. He obviously enjoyed enlightening this

foreign lady. "Only dogs and jungle beasts have white teeth. People chew betel nut. Teeth nice black."

Libby tried to digest this. She had noticed that both their guides had blackened teeth, but she had not realized it was a cultural trait. "I think I understand. And the long ears?"

Njo's black teeth flashed as he grinned. With one dark finger he pointed to her ears. "You have hole in ear."

She nodded. "For earrings."

"My woman wear much earrings. Hang down to shoulders. Make ears long. Very pretty."

"Where is your woman?" Libby asked. "I would like to meet her."

"She stay in village. Live with her people. I live there when not working. Man live in woman's village."

Libby considered this. "Always?"

Njo smiled. "Is *adat*. Boss say *adat* means custom. Everyone obey *adat*." His dark eyes surveyed her. "You have man?"

Libby's face flushed crimson, and she shook her head. "No. I did once."

"What happen?" Njo's dark face was sympathetic.

"We parted."

The guide grinned. "I think maybe you boss woman. White woman no like jungle. You belong boss?"

Libby shook her head. "No, Njo. And I do like the jungle."

It was strange. She had expected to find the rain forest a frightening place. For years she'd read about its dense greenness, the creeping, twisting lianas that festooned the trees, the animals seeking something to devour, the rapid cycle of life to death that existed there. Everything she'd ever read had made it seem rotten and malignant, but she was not seeing it that way.

The mangroves that lined the river banks had a certain dignity. Their twisted, convoluted roots seemed to speak of strength and endurance. Behind them, the taller trees of the rain forest—teak, iron-wood and others—could only be glimpsed. Libby was finding the jungle more mysterious than malevolent. And it possessed a certain wild beauty. Orchids grew freely. She had noted their colorful blooms high up in the trees as the boats moved along the river. Other flowers blossomed, too; exotic flowers for which she had no names clung to tree trunks or exploded from the forest floor.

That was it, she decided. The rain forest was beautiful and mysterious. Something within her responded to it, made her feel an affinity with it. Did men refer to the jungle as *she?* Libby wondered. It seemed to her to be, somehow, feminine.

A sharp cry from the *longbot* ahead made her look up quickly. She followed the wide sweep of Jared's hand. And there, near the edge of the river, stood a village.

"Now you see *lamin*." Njo grinned.

Libby knew she was staring, but she couldn't help it. Njo had said many families, many doors. She had pictured four or six, but this long house had—she counted quickly—some thirty doors. They were passing near enough for her to see the pigs and chickens underneath, a couple of dogs lying in the sun. On the wide, covered veranda men sat talking. And near the river's edge brown-skinned mothers played with laughing, naked babies.

Libby sighed. Once she had thought of babies. Jared's babies. But now that was all lost. There would be no babies at all—no one's—if she couldn't get Jared out of her system.

"Aren't we going to stop?" she said.

Njo shook his head. "Boss have big hurry. We go much far today."

Libby nodded. Jared was setting a hard pace. They had stopped at noon only long enough to eat a scanty lunch.

She leaned back against the *longbot*. She was tired; inactivity could be tiring, too. She wasn't sure if Jared had put her in this boat with Tim to keep her away from Nick or from himself. At any rate she really didn't mind.

To be in the same boat with Jared would be nerve-racking. This way she could relax a little. If she wanted to look at him, she could. And if he looked at her, she at least couldn't feel his gaze so intensely.

It was late afternoon when Jared signaled for them to land. Libby stretched and yawned, glad for the chance to move around, but not wanting to be so close to Jared again. As the *longbots* approached the shore, several shapes disentangled themselves from the green jungle floor and slid into the water.

"Crocs," said Tim nonchalantly. Having dozed for most of the day, he was now wide awake.

Libby suppressed a shudder. They were such ugly-looking things. She recalled her joke with Tim, but at the moment it didn't seem funny.

"Glad we didn't stop at no long house," he remarked, turning his eyes upon her.

"Why? I'd like to see one up close."

Tim shook his head. "Better keep your distance. The people're nice. Real friendly. That's just the trouble."

"I don't understand."

"They'd want us to stay all night. Make room fer us in the long house."

"That seems very hospitable."

Tim laughed. "I reckon it sounds that way. But them long houses is full of fleas. You'd be et up alive."

She saw him grin at her shiver of distaste, and she felt a wave of sadness. Did they all want to see her fail, to drive her back to the States? But then common sense came to her rescue. Tim was just having a little fun.

As Njo nosed the *longbot* into the bank, Tim leaned out and grabbed a protruding root. He tied the boat to it securely, then offered Libby a hand. She didn't hesitate, but put hers in it immediately and, with his help, stepped ashore. She took several steps backward, no more, then stood quietly, waiting for Tim and Njo to join her. She had found the jungle beautiful and mysterious, but she did not intend to forget that it could also be quite dangerous.

Jared had fastened the other *longbot* about twenty feet away. She watched as Nick passed supplies out to him and stepped ashore. The supplies had been stowed in that canoe, and Libby wondered if that was because he thought she might carelessly overturn the one she shared with Tim. She would not ask him about it, of course. She shifted the pack over her shoulder and flexed the muscles in her legs. Sitting so long had made her slightly stiff, but otherwise she felt fine. She was determined to accept whatever came her way. She had no intention of letting anything panic her. Jared would like that, she thought grimly.

Tim and Njo, finished with the *longbot,* moved past her, and she followed. The river made a little inlet here, and beside it someone had cleared some of the jungle floor. The rain forest had already begun to take over again, but Njo and Kustarto, machetes in hand, soon cut a trail a little way into the jungle and cleared a reasonable area.

Libby looked around her. The rain forest was beautiful. The mangroves near the river's edge each seemed to have their own personality. Like bent old women they spread their gnarled roots, so many canes to support themselves. Everything around her was a vibrant, pulsing green. Life was so vivid here, she thought. In the rain forest life's beauty—and its briefness—were both brought forcefully to one's attention.

By this time they had reached a small clearing. She dumped her pack at the spot Jared indicated and then went with the others to gather wood for the fire.

6

~~~~~~~~~~~~~

An hour later found Libby ready to call it quits. A small fire burned in the center of the clearing. Soon the jungle's green twilight would darken, and it would be difficult to see anything beyond the small circle of light that the fire cast. She certainly didn't want to blunder into a crocodile, or something equally ferocious, that might be lurking out there in the darkness.

"Njo!" Jared's voice startled her. She had been studiously avoiding contact with him. "Get Miss Collins a pail of water to wash in."

"Yes, boss," came Njo's cheerful answer.

As she watched the Dayak set out for the river bank with the leather pail, Libby suppressed a shiver. How could he walk so boldly into danger?

She practically held her breath, waiting for his scream to come ripping out of the darkness. But a few minutes later Njo appeared, grinning, with a full pail.

"I wash river," he said, wringing the ends of the *kain* that served as his only garment. "Much water."

"I'll make do here," Libby said calmly, not letting him see that the prospect of a bath in the river didn't exactly thrill her.

Njo nodded. "OK. But river much better."

Libby gazed down into the pail of water. Fortunately, the dim forest light made it seem cleaner than it was. She dipped her hands in its tepidness and lifted them to her face. To her surprise the water felt refreshing. With a sigh she wished she could put her whole body in the bucket. Her khakis were drenched with sweat, and little strands of hair had escaped her braid to cling to her damp face.

"Here." Jared's voice made her jump. The spongy jungle floor had absorbed the sound of his footsteps, and he was standing right behind her.

She turned quickly and found that he was holding a length of deep-blue material covered with pink and white flowers. "Use this."

"What for?" She tried to keep her voice calm and impersonal.

"It's a *kain*. You wear it to wash and sleep in."

For a moment Libby was nonplused. She hadn't the first idea how to use such a thing. And she wasn't going to try with him standing there watching.

But he didn't move away. "Well, put it on." His voice conveyed quite plainly his conception of her as a not-too-smart child.

"I—I think I'll just stay in my khakis," she stammered.

"Nonsense. You can't sleep like—" He stopped suddenly. "Listen, this is a *kain,* a long, narrow length of material. If the two ends were sewn together it would be a sarong. But you couldn't use it as easily. You just wrap it around you and tuck in the top. Instant dress, bathrobe, nightgown, whatever you please. Now get into it. Sleeping in your khakis is out. And I mean it." His eyes raked over her, and she saw their threat. He meant to be obeyed in this.

"Yes, boss," she muttered and was rewarded by a fiercer stare from those gray-green eyes.

"First take your boots off." He saw her hesitation. "You're safe enough here. Nothing's going to come crawling in here looking for your feet."

Libby did as she'd been told, settling on the ground to tug off boots and socks and put them next to her already discarded jungle hat. Then she scrambled to her feet again. She felt better facing him, though he still towered over her.

"Now," he directed, his eyes hard in the dim light. "Wrap the thing around you, up over your shoulders. That way you can take off your shirt. Then you wrap it around and tuck it in over your breasts." His eyes came to rest there and then moved up to her flushed face, but the hard lines of his mouth never softened and she suppressed a shiver. Those eyes were so cold. Implacable.

76

She forced herself to stand steadily, not to drop her eyes. "Thank you. I believe I can manage now."

His eyes stayed on her for a brief moment before he turned away without another comment. For a long moment she stood there, the *kain* draped over her shoulders. Then, realizing that everyone was busying himself at some task or other, she turned her back on them and began the laborious process of getting out of her clothes without losing the *kain*.

Divested of her khakis, she felt suddenly cool and light. The tuck which held up the *kain* made her a little nervous as she knelt carefully beside her knapsack and took out a washcloth and her small cake of soap. A little smile pulled at her lips. She liked the feel of the garment.

It felt wonderfully cool after the heavy, soggy shirt and pants. But there was more to it than that, she thought, as she dampened her cloth in the pail and washed herself. This *kain* made her feel extremely feminine. The way it tucked over her breasts, the way it clung to her body.

With some careful maneuvering she managed to wash her whole body, washing and rinsing, then letting the water evaporate from her bare skin.

By the time she had finished, darkness was closing in. Hanging her cloth on a bush to dry, she put her soap back in its waterproof pouch and took out her comb.

When she turned toward the fire, she saw that only Tim was in the clearing. She moved toward him and the cheerful little flames.

"Looks like you got the hang of it," commented

Tim. His grizzled hair was still wet, and Libby realized he must have taken a dip in the river, too. "Yes," she said. "But it takes practice."

Tim nodded.

Dropping to a log, Libby began to take the pins from her hair. Once she had it combed and rebraided she would feel really herself again. She let the braids fall to her shoulders and loosened her hair.

"Mighty pretty stuff," said Tim.

"Thank you." Libby combed carefully, loosening the tangles. Finally her hair lay in a golden cloud on her bare shoulders. She would braid it up again, but for a moment she sat quiet, resting, staring at the fire.

A noise beyond the circle of light made her head snap erect. Into the fire glow came a tall, dark man, a *kain* wrapped around his lean hips. Libby's breath caught in her throat. At first she had almost mistaken Jared for a native. His chest and legs were almost as darkly bronzed as his face. Did he follow his own advice? she wondered, as he strode toward her across the little clearing. If she hadn't been along, would he have spent the whole trip barefoot in a *kain*?

She looked up at him, looming there above her in the firelight. Water still dripped from his dark hair and glistened in the curling black mat on his chest. He looked mysterious, dangerous. Oh-so-attractive. Her blood was pounding and she wondered how she looked to him, clad in the *kain* and with her hair spread out. She caught herself wishing she had stuck a wildflower behind her ear. But then she was glad she hadn't. He might think she was trying to make herself attractive to him.

"Feeling more comfortable?"

Libby barely prevented herself from starting. Her concentration had been so centered on Jared that she hadn't even noticed Nick coming up behind him. Water dripped from him, too, but he was wearing a pair of cutoffs—whether for her benefit or because he didn't want to go native, she had no way of knowing.

"Yes, Nick." She gave him a bright smile. "I'm beginning to think the people here have the right idea. This is very comfortable."

Nick nodded, but she could see he was uneasy about something.

"Where's that repellent?" Jared asked, his voice resounding in the small clearing.

"Over there by my knapsack," said Tim. "Better bring some for Libby again."

Jared nodded. He spent a few minutes rubbing himself with the stuff, then he retraced his steps, coming to a stop before her. His powerful thighs were level with her eyes and the sight of them raised a flood of feeling in her. But before she could raise her eyes to his, he had moved around her.

"I'll put it on your back."

Even before she could reply, his fingers were on her skin, warm, strong fingers. Her flesh quivered under their touch. He was taunting her, she knew. He was reminding her that he could arouse her body at will.

As his fingers slid over her shoulders and down toward the swell of her breasts, she sucked in her breath. His touch was soft, light, so innocent in the eyes of the watching men, but so arousing to her. And Jared knew it. She was sure of that, she thought, as she forced herself to sit quietly.

He put repellent on her bare arms and then moved

around in front of her. "Now for your legs," he said evenly, as he pushed the *kain* up to her knees.

"I can do it." She hadn't meant to speak, to give him that satisfaction, but she couldn't help herself. Having him touch her like that was pure torture. That was why he was doing it, of course.

His tone was light as he replied, but his eyes were cold and hard. "Better let me handle it. Those *kains* can be tricky to bend over in."

Her hands went automatically to her breasts, and she flushed as Tim chuckled. There was no use in protesting. She could see that. She would just have to grit her teeth and bear it. His hands caressed her legs, lingering on her instep, which he had learned long ago was one of her most erotic zones. Desire raced through her.

From near the fire came the sharp clatter of a dropping pan. Tim might think the boss was just having a little fun, but Nick knew better. Libby saw it in the glance he gave her as he stooped to retrieve the pan.

Jared realized it, too. For he got to his feet and turned to hand the bottle to Nick. "You'll be wanting some of this, too."

There was the briefest hesitation on Nick's part before he took the proffered bottle. "Thanks."

Libby was at the wrong angle to see Nick's face or Jared's as this exchange took place, but she caught the hesitation. What was Jared conveying to Nick by the look in his eyes? She sighed and began to braid up her hair again. Things were getting more and more complicated.

* * *

An hour later Libby settled down on her sleeping bag, pulling shut the mosquito net that Njo had rigged for her. At night the jungle lost a great deal of its beauty for her. It was so black beyond the circle of firelight, black and dangerous-looking. Now that they were no longer talking, many sounds came to her from that darkness. Grunts and snorts and distant growls punctuated the background drone made by the myriad insects.

The fire had burned down to glowing embers, casting very little light, and the great jungle trees towering around their little clearing cut off the sight of the night sky.

Libby sighed. She was not used to sleeping like this, out in the open. It was far too warm to get inside her bag. She wiggled around, trying to get comfortable, and the *kain* twisted over her hips and pulled across her breasts. If only she had a thin sheet or something to cover herself with, she would take it off. Then she smiled. Untucking the top of the *kain,* she lifted her hips, slid one side out from under her. It took only seconds to arrange the long piece of material like a sheet.

She lay back down again and tried to relax. She was tired, though not exhausted. Traveling by water was not as physically tiring as walking, and this part of the river was wide. There would be rapids to be portaged later on, Njo had told her, and that accounted for the Spartan nature of their supplies and the fact that they would be living mostly off river fish. When everything had to be carried around the rapids, it was important to consider weight.

Jared was a good boss, she thought. He knew how

to handle men. But not women, said her mind. That was not strictly true, of course. Jared did know how to handle women. And the word "handle" was the right one here. Once he got his hands on her, she couldn't help wanting him. Beneath the thin *kain* her body began to tremble.

She wanted him now. It was practically impossible not to after seeing him all day in the other *longbot* and sitting by the fire while they ate their rations. Desire pulsed through her. When he had put the repellent on her, his touch had filled her with fierce longing. He was hard and even cruel sometimes, but he always had good reason. Or thought he had. Nick and Tim both admired him, and Njo's admiration extended almost to worship.

Perhaps he was only cruel to her, she thought, because he'd been hurt. It seemed clear that the break-up of their marriage *had* hurt him. He was certainly very bitter about it. She twisted under the flowered *kain*. He had a right to be bitter. But she was sorry for what she'd done, for the foolish mistakes she'd made in her immaturity. She hadn't set out to hurt him deliberately. And she'd been hurt herself. But now she had to sleep. She had to be alert to-morrow.

Using the relaxation techniques she had learned in school, Libby managed to fall asleep. Her last thought was of Jared, of his dark face and those green-gray eyes staring at her.

She wakened sometime later, her body rigid. At first she hardly knew where she was. But a sound came out of the darkness. In the blackness something was moving. She heard no more noise, but she could feel—she could feel the thing getting closer.

Her heart was pounding heavily in her chest. There were tigers in this jungle. Tigers and many other kinds of wild animals. A shiver sped over her. Was that a tiger out there? She strained, her eyes peering into the darkness.

The sound came again, this time closer and Libby sat upright, the *kain* that covered her forgotten in her terror. She couldn't just lie there and let some jungle beast maul her. But if it was a figment of her imagination, she didn't want to wake the others.

She grabbed wildly at the netting that surrounded her. If only she wasn't so far away from the rest of them.

Her breath was coming in great gasps now, and her heart seemed to be in her mouth.

Suddenly the netting was pulled aside and a powerful pair of arms came around her. Though the darkness made seeing anything impossible, she knew immediately that it was Jared whose arms enfolded her, who was gathering her trembling body against his own hard one. The meeting of her flesh with his shocked some of the fear out of her. The *kain* had fallen to her waist when she sat up, and her bare breasts were pressed against his naked chest. The scent of him was in her nostrils. Her terror began slowly to fade. Jared would protect her. There was no need to be afraid.

As the panic receded, it was replaced by something else. The feel of his body against her own was raising desire in her. In spite of all her resolutions, she wanted him. The feel of him against her was driving her mad. Without thinking, she raised her face to his.

It was very dark. The dying glow of the fire didn't reach this far, and she could not see his face. She felt the momentary stiffening of his body as her lips touched his chin, and then his mouth came down on hers. She did not think of rejecting him. She could not.

At first his kiss was soft, gentle, as though it meant to be comforting, but Libby was no longer thinking of the jungle. It, and any danger that might come from it, had left her consciousness. There was room there only for Jared, for the wonderful feel of his body. She opened her lips to his probing tongue, welcoming the feel of it against the sensitive inside of her lips.

His kiss was changing. From one of comfort it was becoming one of arousal. Then his arms shifted, and he was lowering her back on the sleeping bag, his body lying beside hers.

Silently there in the darkness his hands moved over her body. Libby bit her lip to keep back a moan. She didn't want Nick or Tim to know about this.

Her arms went up around Jared's neck. This was the old Jared—the one who had taught her the joys of womanhood, the one who had wakened her body to the glories of love.

The darkness and the silence added a dreamlike quality to their lovemaking. Perhaps she *was* dreaming, Libby thought as his hands caressed her breasts, coaxed each nipple to a swollen peak. She had dreamed of him so many times in the last years, dreamed that he was loving her in the old wonderful ways.

His breath was warm on her ear as he kissed it.

Then his lips moved across her bare shoulder, down the valley between her breasts. She blinked rapidly to keep back the sudden tears. It was like this that he had made love to her after their arguments—gently, tenderly—coaxing her into a submission so complete that it had sometimes frightened her.

But she was stronger now, she told herself. And, had Jared only known it, there was no need to coax. She wanted him. She had wanted him for the last seven years. She admitted this to herself as his hands threw the *kain* aside and his mouth moved across her flat belly. She did not want to get him out of her life. She wanted to get him back in it—permanently.

Her hands crept to his shoulders, to the matted hair on his chest. The truth was that she still loved Jared Harper. She had never stopped loving him. She tried to tell him that with her silently moving fingers as she caressed his firm, hard body.

His hands left her for a moment, and her heart rose up in her throat. He couldn't mean to leave her like this! But then she heard the soft rustle of material and knew that he was loosening the swath of material around his own hips.

Then his body was on hers. Only his mouth covering hers kept her from uttering the moan that gathered at the back of her throat as she opened herself to him.

Slowly, there in the tropical darkness, he moved against her, each thrust of his body against hers driving her further into a world of hazy ecstasy. It had to be love, she told herself, that made it so good with Jared. She loved him. She could see that now. It was because of her love for him that no one else had been able to strike a spark in her over all those long years.

There had been men, many men, wanting to try. But something had always held her back. Their kisses had not affected her as Jared's had. She had let them go so far, hoping. But when nothing had happened to her inside, she'd drawn the line. And now she was here, in the middle of East Kalimantan, with Jared, and she knew that no other man would ever do for her.

He stopped suddenly, resting part of his weight on his elbows, and she felt his lips against her ear. It was like this that he had teased her in those long-ago days, stopping to let her body move against his. She did so now, her hips arching up eagerly, even though she had not consciously meant to move. He knew her body so well, he knew exactly how to please her.

Her hands moved across the hard muscles of his back. His body had not changed much over the years. It had always been lean and hard. Her hands came up to clutch at his shoulders. His mouth covered hers again, muffling the cries that she usually uttered at the moment of rapture. And then it swept over her, washing her with waves of ecstasy, before letting her come to rest in a pool of sweet contentment. She felt the signals that told her that he, too, had known that tumultuous moment of fulfillment, and she smiled.

But her contentment vanished as she felt his body leaving hers. She heard the slight sound as his groping hand found his discarded *kain,* and then he was gone as silently as he had come.

The jungle night was still warm, but Libby began to shiver uncontrollably. He had not even kissed her afterward, had not even touched her cheek. He had simply picked himself up and walked off. Left her there, like something he had used and no longer needed, she told herself bitterly.

She felt about in the darkness until she located her *kain*. Rising to her feet, she wrapped it around her. She had to talk to him. Now.

She frowned, trying to remember. His bag had been about a quarter of the way around the circle from hers, between hers and the men, she realized suddenly. She began to move in that direction, her bare feet soundless.

The moon was visible for a few seconds, illuminating the clearing briefly before it was covered by another cloud. In that time she saw his bag and moved toward him. He had put his bag closer to the fire, and as she drew near she could make out the outline of his mosquito net.

She approached slowly and knelt beside him. The shape under the net was not moving, and his breathing was slow and steady. "Jared!" she pleaded. "Please, we've got to talk."

There was no answer from the still shape under the netting.

"Jared!" She thought of touching him, of trying to shake him awake. It seemed inconceivable that he could have fallen asleep so soon. In the old days they had always talked afterward. Their contented bodies comfortably entwined, they had found their differences and squabbles so much silliness and returned to their lovemaking with renewed vigor. They had not really solved their problems, she could see that now. But they had thought they had and things had been good between them again. For a while, at least.

She had expected it to be that way tonight, hoped

that in the whispered confidences of love's aftermath she might convince him that she had changed. But he was determined to give her no such opportunity.

Their lovemaking had not been that for him. He had used her, and—though it was gently and with tenderness—the effect was the same. She *felt* used. It was a feeling she did not like at all, she thought as she crept back to her place and tried to relax.

But relaxation and sleep were far from her. Jared's behavior didn't change the revelation that she had had during their union. She still loved Jared Harper. To all intents and purposes she was still Jared Harper's wife. Without him, her life was empty.

She stared up into the darkness. Yes, she loved Jared. Loved him as much, maybe even more, than she had seven years ago. Why couldn't he love her? That he wanted her was plain to see. But wanting needn't be connected to love—wanting could be pure lust.

If only she could make him love her again. But how could she *make* a man love her? Especially Jared, whose love she had so effectively destroyed by accusing him of things he had probably never even done. Jared might have knocked around a lot in his life, but he had a high sense of honor. It was not like him to have cheated on her. Any more than it was likely she would have done that to him.

He might still believe that she had, of course. Accusations had flown fast and furious that last night. In her desire to hurt him as she had been hurt she had said many things—some of which she no longer remembered. But she would never have considered loving anyone else. She had belonged to him—body and soul. And she still did.

The thought was chilling, but it did no good to deny the truth. She had done that for too many years. There had to be a better way. Her mind circled round and round, always coming back to the same thing. If only he loved her . . .

7

⠿⠿⠿⠿⠿⠿⠿⠿⠿

The next morning Libby woke to the clatter of pans. Tim was busy over the fire with breakfast, and the rest of them were nowhere to be seen. She sat up, clutching the *kain* to her as she belatedly realized her nakedness beneath it.

"Boss had 'em put a pail of water over there fer you," Tim said over his shoulder. "They went down to the river to wash."

The memory of last night came sweeping back to Libby. Had Tim heard them? Did he know what had happened? His voice didn't sound any different. The best thing was to act normal.

She stretched, still holding the *kain*. She felt hot and sticky. "Why can't I go swimming, too?" she asked, pushing back the netting.

"'Cause they ain't got no clothes on."

She stopped, halfway to her feet, arrested by the thought of seeing Jared like that, naked in the water, cavorting with the guides like some carefree child. She pushed herself erect. "The pail doesn't hold enough water," she complained.

Tim shrugged. "Better talk to the boss. He's the one gives the orders. Guess he thought you wouldn't like washing in the river. With crocs 'n' snakes 'n' all." He looked at her slyly.

Libby shook her head. "You don't fool me, you old devil." She gave him a grin. "If the snakes and crocs were that bad, the men wouldn't be there either." She pulled the *kain* tight and tucked it in. "I'm going down there. I want a swim."

"Best call out then," Tim said soberly. "The boss ain't gonna like being caught in his birthday suit. Nor the others either."

Libby felt the rising anger. Last night Jared had used her. Now he expected her to wash in a small pail of water. It was unfair. Besides, she was hot and sticky. The thought of a dip in the river was immensely appealing. And it couldn't be that dangerous. Every long house they'd passed had had laughing children playing at the water's edge. Why shouldn't she enjoy a morning dip just like everyone else?

She could hear the splashing as she drew near the river. If Jared had been there alone, she would have thrown caution to the wind and gone to meet him without revealing her presence first. Then she would have made him talk—about last night and the two of them. But Nick and the guides *were* with him, and so she sang out, "Nick, I'm coming to the river."

The splashing stopped. "Wait a minute." Jared's voice came booming back to her. She could hear them moving around. Then Jared called, "All right, come on."

She made her way around the curve of jungle greenery. Nick and Jared stood on the bank. Their hair and their bodies were dripping wet, but Nick's cutoffs and Jared's *kain* were only partly damp.

"I didn't mean to spoil your fun," she said with a smile at Nick. "I just thought a dip in the river would be refreshing."

Nick's answering smile came quickly, but Jared's expression remained sober. "There are crocs and water snakes in the river," Jared said. "I didn't think you'd want to go in."

"But I do," Libby replied quickly, not meeting his eyes. It couldn't be as dangerous as he was making out.

He sighed as though pampering a spoiled child. "All right then. But just five minutes. We've got to get moving."

Because they were both watching her, Libby plunged boldly into the river. Even this early in the day the water wasn't cool. But it was wet and felt very good.

She swam back and forth across the small expanse of water, ducked under and opened her eyes, enjoying the even dimmer greenness of this underwater world. With determination she ignored the men standing there and swam and floated until Jared's voice came to her, "Time's up."

Shaking the water from her eyes, she stood. Until that moment she had been more or less unconscious of the *kain,* but now, heavy with water, it pulled across her breasts. The rest of it was plastered against her body, leaving very little to the imagination.

"That should hold me till we stop tonight," she said, ignoring Jared's survey of her body. She could play this as cool as he could. "From now on I'd like to swim with the rest of you." Her eyes met his in a direct challenge. "If you don't mind."

Jared shrugged his bronze shoulders. "Of course. You're an equal member of the team."

His stress on the word "equal" contradicted his meaning, but she decided to ignore that. "Thank you," she replied sweetly.

Something almost like amusement flickered in his eyes, and she wondered what further annoyances he had planned for her. But it didn't matter, she told herself with determination, because whatever Jared tried *she* wasn't going to cry quits.

She stepped out of the river then, the dripping material still clinging to her body, and started back toward the clearing. Jared might snipe at her, but he was an inherently fair man. If she could just hold out, really pull her weight, he would have to admit that he was wrong, that she *was* an effective member of the team. Then he would have to see that she'd grown up.

She felt his eyes on her as she moved up the path ahead of him. How did he feel after last night? she wondered. It had always been hard to guess his feelings. His face was usually set in hard lines and his eyes clouded. Except when they were making love. His face had softened then, and his eyes had become warm and loving. Would he ever look at her that way again? she wondered. Or was his bitterness too great to be overcome?

She reached the camp and realized suddenly that wearing a wet *kain* could complicate the problem of getting dressed.

She was puzzling over this when Nick appeared beside her. He was holding a long length of deep-green material covered with pale yellow flowers. "I didn't think you'd need this," he said, his eyes staying carefully on her face, "since Jared gave you one. But it might come in handy now."

Libby looked at the *kain*. "I appreciate your thoughtfulness," she said. "But I don't quite understand how it will help."

Nick's grin was sheepish. "I'll show you." He turned his back on her. "Now," he said over his shoulder as he stretched out his arms, "open the *kain*. Put one end in each of my hands. Presto, instant dressing room."

Libby chuckled. "You're a very innovative man, Nick." She followed his instructions.

The curtain wasn't exactly the ultimate in privacy, but it certainly beat trying to find a place in the jungle, she thought as she hurried into her clothes.

"Thank you, kind sir." She took the *kain* from his outstretched hands, carefully avoiding Jared's eyes. She didn't need to be stared at anymore. Their lovemaking was extremely vivid in her mind without having his eyes linger on her.

Nick turned, smiling. "I figured there might be some difficulty in giving you privacy," he said. "So I just used my imagination."

Libby nodded and would have said more, but Jared's voice echoed through the camp. "Let's get moving. We've wasted enough time."

With a quick glance at Nick, Libby dropped to the ground and began pulling on her socks and boots. It would only take a minute to repack her knapsack. Then she'd be ready.

An hour later they were back on the river, only this time Jared had put Tim in the canoe with Nick and was sharing hers. He sat there, his eyes intent on the river while Njo guided the *longbot*.

"We stop Tenggaron, boss?" the guide asked.

Jared shook his head. "No, our work is further up river."

"Lady maybe like see rajah's palace." Njo's dark eyes glittered at some private joke.

"I doubt that," Jared replied dryly, his eyes never leaving the wide expanse of the river before them.

"Why wouldn't I like it?" Libby asked.

Jared shrugged. "The rajah has twenty wives."

"Twenty!" She couldn't help the surprise in her voice.

"Another evidence of a different culture," Jared replied. "The rajah's in his seventies now," he continued. "Lives in the palace. At least the Dutchman who built it in the Thirties considered it a palace. The rajah has opened the place to the people as a museum. He has some great Ming china." He turned and his eyes met hers. "Also some Hindu sculptures from the cave in Gua Kembang. In the bedroom, of course."

She didn't need Njo's laughter to understand the nature of those sculptures. That it was definitely sexual was reflected in Jared's glance.

"Town old," Njo contributed. "Look good in morning. Mist. No see good then."

Jared laughed. "You can judge for yourself." He pointed to the old wooden town that was now coming into view on the river bank.

Libby gazed at it entranced. It was bigger than the ramshackle villages they had passed the day before.

The morning mist was fading, but enough of it lingered around the town to partly mask the peeling of some of the pastel-painted houses and the gray weathering of the others. Libby didn't mind their age. The town looked romantic and unreal, like something out of a fantasy painting. "It's lovely," she whispered, her voice falling automatically.

Jared didn't turn to her, but the eloquent shrug of his shoulders was proof enough of his scorn. Was there nothing left that could touch him? she wondered. Had the failure of their marriage so embittered him that he could no longer see beauty anywhere?

"How soon do we get down to work?" she asked as the fairylike town faded into the distance behind them.

"A few days yet. We need to get beyond the generally traveled area."

"I see."

"In the meantime"—he reached down to the waterproof case at his feet—"you might take a gander at these." And he handed her a roll of maps and reports.

Libby spent the next days studying. Every time she believed she had mastered all he'd given her, Jared reached down into his case and extracted something else.

By the time the river had narrowed and Jared began their actual surveying work, she was quite ready for physical activity. Having him in the same boat with her had not made the studying any easier either. He was always so close. She could have reached out and touched the hard muscles in his back. She didn't, of course. Since that night he had taken her in silence and darkness, she had put her sleeping bag near the others.

It was not that she didn't want him, she told herself as she followed him ashore at the place he had chosen for the first series of tests. Every morning and evening when they took their swims, she had trouble keeping her eyes off him. His body was so familiar to her; she knew it almost better than she knew her own. But she didn't want a repeat of that experience in the darkness that had left her feeling used.

She wasn't going to think about that now, however. There was work to be done here. From her study of the maps it appeared that practically half of Kalimantan was sitting over the continental shelf. But they must still find the basins and troughs with thick sediment where adequate structural traps lay. For without the structural traps to hold it, the oil would have seeped away over the centuries. Marine exploration and discovery, of the kind that took place on the shelf when it extended around the outer edge of a land mass, was normally more expensive than that on land. But here in the jungle, with the difficulty of transportation, it might be a different case.

A picture of the rigs along the coast at Balikpapan

rose in her mind. That there was oil around here was certainly indicated, but finding it would be another story. Of course the oil offshore in Balikpapan was also from the continental shelf, and she supposed that most of the river mouths had already been investigated. The huge masses of sediment brought down by a river into a delta, a relatively restricted area, often led to the formation of large quantities of oil.

But their task was with the interior, and it was a formidable task. The usual procedure in the States—of sending in some trucks with a seismographic crew—would obviously not work here. It could take many many months for a crew to make much progress, cutting its way through vast areas of wild rain forest. It could take a week to get one reading.

Clearly what they were doing was more feasible. Scouting the area, they would look for signs. Not just the readily apparent oil seepages—which could be extremely difficult to evaluate, because the very fact of seepage could indicate that most of the oil was already gone—but other more subtle hints, like the quality of the surface sand or rock.

When they did start, the seismographic crew would have quite a job, she thought. It was true that there were helicopters. But where would a copter land in this tangled mass of jungle? Well, that was not her worry. They were only supposed to scout out and record the most promising locations. The next crew would do the seismographic stuff and drill some boreholes for stratigraphic tests. That was recognized now as a good way of charting, though once it had been frowned upon. Libby wondered idly how many more oil fields would have been in production if the value of such test holes had been discovered sooner.

"This is a good spot," Jared said suddenly, coming to a stop.

Libby stopped, too, and unslung her pack.

"Get us a reading here and put up a marker," Jared said to Tim. "We'll be here for a day or two. You each know your jobs."

Libby and Nick nodded. Her hand went automatically to her own waterproof case. Her copies of the topographic maps were there, the maps she was to make notations on. And the notebooks in which she would make her recommendations. It would be good to be working again, in this very concrete way, instead of just studying someone else's information. And this job was in a different kind of location. Most of her previous work had been done in the sandy, rocky, dry areas around Texas and Oklahoma. Here everything was wet and swampy. The experience would look good in her dossier.

Jared consulted his watch, then looked at the sky. "We've got a couple hours of daylight left. Let's use them."

Njo and Kustarto began immediately to clear an area for the camp. Nick and Tim turned to their packs and began setting up the survey equipment.

Libby looked around her. The river bank might be a good place to begin. The erosion caused by the water there would reveal some of the subsurface strata of the underlying rock structure.

"Libby."

She looked up, meeting Jared's eyes. "Yes?"

"Don't go too far from camp. This isn't Texas." He nodded toward the green tangle of trees and vines outside the small clearing. "It's easy to get lost out there. And the pythons and rhinos won't care that you're a woman."

"I have my compass," Libby said. "Besides, I never get lost."

"Good," Jared replied. "Because we haven't got the time to waste looking for you."

"Yes, sir. I know." Libby made her tone calm. Jared was her boss: He had the right to give her orders. And flaring up at him, no matter how good it might feel at the moment, would only convince him that he was right that she wasn't able to handle a job like this.

His eyes searched her face for long moments before he turned and left her. Suppressing a sigh, she gathered up her things and started for the river bank. She was much less frightened by the jungle now and more and more impressed with its wild and primitive beauty.

"Be sure to stand aside and call them crocs 'grandfather' like the natives do," Tim called after her.

"I'll send them up to get you," she retorted with a grin. If she saw any crocs, she wasn't planning to stick around for conversation. But by now she had realized what the others already knew. The animals in the rain forest, by and large, were no more eager to meet humans than the humans were to meet them. It was more or less a case of live and let live, she thought. Nevertheless, she walked carefully and paid serious attention to any log that looked like it might suddenly sprout legs and teeth and waddle toward her.

She stood near the shallows of the river. At each end of the small inlet where the *longbots* were moored a bank jutted out, its exposed edge beckoning to her.

Libby considered. She could see the sand in the bottom of the shallows. It seemed safe enough, nothing lurking there. She took off her boots and socks and rolled up her trousers. A little wading seemed called for here.

The water was tepid, of course. But she no longer minded that. Tonight, when they came down to take their baths, she would bring her khakis and wash them out. The river was not particularly clean, but then neither were her clothes.

She moved closer to the exposed ledge and began taking notes. Beginning at the top, she worked her way downward, recording each layer. Time passed quickly, and the light was beginning to fade as she drew nearer to the water level, making it difficult to see. She hunkered down, the seat of her pants only inches above the water that lapped at her ankles.

Completely lost in her work, she had nevertheless been listening unconsciously for any strange sound. The sudden sharp snap of a twig from somewhere on the bank nearby startled her so that she lost her balance and fell over backward into the water. The shallows were not very deep, but falling backward as she did, she automatically raised her arms to protect her notes, with the result that practically all the rest of her went under. She rolled quickly, an automatic reflex, coming to her knees and facing the direction of the sound.

She shook the water from her eyes and looked up.

There, towering over her, stood Jared. The hard impassivity of his face remained fixed, except for one corner of his mouth which twitched with what was probably repressed amusement.

"Hello," he said. "Sorry I startled you. I hope your notes didn't get damaged."

Water ran down her back and between her breasts. It dripped from her hair. Libby glanced down at the pad in her hand. She had learned long ago to use only waterproof ink. The page showed a few water spots, but it was still readable.

She got slowly to her feet. "No, the notes are fine. And a little wetness won't hurt me either."

He nodded, his eyes moving slowly over her. "Tim said you'd come this way. Over an hour ago."

He paused, and a shiver of anticipation ran over her. Why must he look at her like that?

"I thought maybe you'd decided to take your swim early."

She said the first thing that came to her mind. "I didn't bring my *kain.*"

He shrugged. "The best suit is none at all."

She felt the heat flooding over her. Had he come down here, so quietly without calling out, hoping to find her naked? She had a quick vision of the two of them, nude, playing and splashing in the shallows, making passionate love in the sand where he stood.

She had to swallow twice before she could speak, but she was pleased when her voice came out cool and collected. "No, boss. I was just working."

He nodded. "I saw that. You were really concentrating. What if I'd been a croc or a tiger?"

"I don't believe tigers like water," she replied, stepping out onto the bank. "And I *was* listening. That's why I reacted so strongly to the noise you made."

His eyes were cloudy as she drew near him, and she couldn't read their expression. She was almost past him when he grabbed her by the waist and swung her around to face him. "Libby!" Desire was plain in his eyes then; she felt her own rising to meet it. But she had to resist him, had to make him understand that she was not just another body to be used.

It was easier to think these things than to say them. His hands were warm on her waist, and he pulled her toward him hungrily. She knew then that she'd been right. He had hoped to find her naked.

"Libby, I want you." His voice was low and husky. Her pulse pounded. If only they could go back in time . . . If only they could start over . . .

She shook her head. "It's no good, Jared." The words were just a whisper. "I don't want—"

His descending mouth cut off the rest of her sentence. It was not a gentle kiss. He made no attempt at persuasion. He simply took what he wanted, hungrily, greedily, crushing her against the long length of him, entirely impervious to her wet clothing.

She tried to push him away, tried to escape his demanding lips, but he was too strong for her. His kiss tore the breath from her, left her weak in the knees. Still, when he finally released her mouth, she shook her head. "No, Jared. I'm part of the survey crew, nothing more. I don't intend to be used."

The desire left his eyes and was replaced by anger.

"If I'm a user, it's because I learned it from you," he said harshly. "You're the queen of users. From that first day that you saw me in the fields—"

"No, Jar—"

But he didn't let her finish. His eyes were hard, green daggers ripping at her. "You used me, and when you found someone else you dumped me."

Astonishment kept her from speaking. All these years he had really believed that!

"But I know you, Libby. I know what you need." His face twisted savagely and she gasped as his hands tightened on her waist. "And I'm warning you. Stay away from my crew. If you need a man"—his lips curved in a sneer—"as I'm sure you do, then come to me. I don't want my crew messed up by your *femme fatale* tactics."

He glared down at her, his face hard and uncompromising, and she tried to marshal the words to convince him. But no words would come. He thought that she had never loved him, that she had cheated on him. And his bitterness had kept him from seeing anything else. It had warped his vision of her—and of the world—her stunned mind told her. So that he was incapable of even noticing that she had changed.

"I would like to remind you," she said, keeping her voice as cool as she could, "that I was *working* when you came down here. I think even you would have to admit that I do my job. And I do it well."

She met his hard gaze fearlessly, though her heart was pounding in her throat.

His eyes blazed. Hot, green fires, she told herself hazily. The hands that spanned her waist tightened. She saw his mouth move, almost as though he meant to kiss her, and then he was shaking her instead, his face a mask of conflicting anger and desire. "Don't push me too far, Libby!" he cried angrily. "I mean what I say. Leave my men alone!"

He released her then, spinning on his heel and stalking off so quickly that he didn't see her slowly crumple to the earth, her legs temporarily unable to support her suddenly trembling body, her eyes filled with hot tears.

8

The days passed. Libby spent them in the *longbot*, sitting behind a silent Jared, or somewhere near an established camp, doing what she'd come to do. As much as she could, she kept to herself, trying for a reserved friendliness that would keep Jared from casting her accusing glances.

The words he had said there by the river were burned into her soul. If it hadn't been so awful, it might have been funny—Jared accusing her of having slept around when all the time the memory of being with him had kept her from any other man. But it wasn't funny, because he had branded her—branded her as some loose, low woman who would take any man she could get. No wonder he had allowed himself to use her as he had. Such a woman deserved no respect in his eyes, and he gave her none.

The days grew into weeks, and their progress up the river, though slow, was consistent. The river had narrowed considerably, Libby thought, the day Long-bagun faded into the distance behind them. Now it narrowed even more, the rain forest almost growing out over it. Mangroves leaned far into the water, their roots reaching out in all directions to give them support. Giant orchids and other flowers imparted a wild, exotic beauty to the jungle that Libby had begun—a fact surprising even to herself—to love.

At night, close to the others, she listened to the croaks of the tropical bullfrogs, the now-familiar sounds of the jungle, and watched the gaily flitting fireflies.

By day she kept an eye out for rare birds and animals. Looking for kingfishers and rhinobirds, for the peacocklike *tumbau* bird and for other brightly feathered denizens of the rain forest made the long day trips up river more interesting and helped her keep her mind off Jared. So far they had not actually seen any jungle animals except the crocs, but they had heard them in the distance. They had seen snakes, but Libby had kept her courage. A python draped from the branch of a tree was no longer a fearful sight, nor the rustling of leaves necessarily a cause for alarm. Even the crocs sunning themselves on the banks had come to be commonplace, though respected, features of the river.

But there were other things to be faced now that

they'd passed Longbagun. The rapids, the narrow, dangerous rapids Njo had told her about, were to be found beyond Longbagun.

"Water bad. We walk," he had said. "Carry boat. More quick."

Libby had already decided on what she would carry. She was fully determined to keep up her end, to do her share of the work. More than once Nick had tried to help her, but she had warned him away with a glance. If she expected to have any chance of changing Jared's mind, she had to do everything for herself.

The ground around the first portage looked rough, but the rapids looked even rougher. Libby shouldered her pack and scrambled ashore, grabbing Jared's pack and the waterproof case that held the maps and charts from the pile of things on the bank. She saw Jared's look of surprise, but she ignored it. The supplies were in the other canoe, and Nick and Tim would have to take care of them. But she intended to do all she could. Without waiting for the others, she went off after the first canoe, keeping herself to a steady pace.

Tim and Nick were both wearing packs, and Kustarto was, too. The Dayak made a strange figure as he wielded his machete through the tangled vines and creepers by the riverside, the bright-orange pack contrasting sharply with his dark-brown skin and the blue-black tattoos that decorated it; but the pack in no way interfered with his task. Nor did the packs the others were wearing seem to hamper them.

Libby paused beside the two extra packs Nick and Tim had left behind, the packs that held supplies. Jared's pack swung from one of her shoulders and the waterproof case from the other, but she might be able to carry one of these in her arms.

"Get moving, Libby." Jared had come up without her seeing him.

"But these packs—" she protested, turning partway toward him.

"You're carrying enough already." Was that the faintest note of admiration in his voice? She wasn't sure, and his face betrayed nothing of what he was thinking or feeling as he and Njo shrugged into the remaining packs and shouldered their *longbot*.

She hadn't gone far when she realized that she simply couldn't have handled anything else. Both her hands had to be free. The trail Kustarto cut was very narrow, and there were swinging lianas and hanging branches to push out of the way as well as the severed greenery that covered the ground and threatened to trip her up. The packs grew heavier and heavier, but she kept up the pace.

Ahead of her she could hear Kustarto's cheerful grunts as he hacked away at the jungle growth. Behind him, and just ahead of her on the trail, Tim and Nick balanced the first *longbot* on their shoulders. And behind her, though she did not take the energy to turn and look, Jared and Njo were bringing the second.

She kept her eyes on the trail. One wrong step would put her in a heap on the ground, and Jared would be assured of her incompetence. Grimly she put one boot after the other. The packs were heavy, and they grew heavier with each step. Her shoulders began to ache; a sharp pain settled in the small of her back. Her shirt and pants were both wet, clinging to her sweaty skin. Sweat trickled down the valley between her breasts and beaded her upper lip. But she refused to look at her watch. Njo had told her that the portages took about an hour. This one had to end eventually. She plodded doggedly on.

It was some time later when Libby grew aware that something had changed. At first she didn't know what. Then it came to her, Kustarto's grunts and cries had stopped. He was no longer cutting trail. Tim and Nick took a turn in the path, and when she followed them she found they were lowering their *longbot* back into the river.

Relief washed over her. She had done her part. A noise behind her announced the arrival of Jared and Njo.

Tim cleared a section of sand and sank down. "Who's going back for the other stuff?" he asked.

"No one." Jared's voice held obvious satisfaction. Libby recognized it with a brief flaring of joy. "Everything's here."

It was only then that Tim saw Libby. She saw his eyes widen as he took in the extra packs she was carrying.

"Come on." Jared's voice was even as they lowered the *longbot* back into the water. "We haven't got time to waste."

Obediently Libby moved to the water's edge. And when Njo took Jared's pack and the map case from her, his dark eyes showed admiration. Plainly, the boss had given this foreign woman his approval.

Staring at the shirt stretched across his broad back, Libby smiled slightly. Jared hadn't failed to notice that she had done her share. No one had had to return for the supply packs that Jared and Njo had been able to bring because *she* had carried the other things.

They spent two more hours on the river. The intertwining branches and strangler figs overhead reached clear across the narrow expanse of water, forming a green tunnel and filtering out most of the sunlight. Sometimes tendrils hung down almost into the boat. Once Libby reached up and picked a wild orchid.

She held it for some time, admiring its intricate beauty as she admired that of the wild and teeming jungle around them. But Jared seemed to see nothing of that. He cared only for business. The multitude of beautiful blossoms, the bright-feathered exotic birds, all meant nothing to him. He had only one thing on his mind: oil.

With a small sigh Libby put the orchid on top of her pack. Her efforts to reach him seemed almost futile. Jared was so changed. So hard and bitter that she wondered if anyone would ever get through to him again. He had encased himself in a shell much harder than the one he had worn when she first met him. It hurt to know that she was responsible, in part at least, for his cynical attitude toward women. But she had not meant to hurt him. Why couldn't he see that? Why couldn't he understand that she'd been hurt, too? They were both to blame for the failure of their marriage. She was more than willing to concede that. But she wasn't willing to take *all* the blame. And she certainly wasn't willing to be labeled the way he insisted on labeling her.

The canoe nosed into land, and Libby had to

abandon her thoughts. Each of them had things to do to set up camp. There was no time for regrets about the past or problems with no apparent solutions.

By this time they had established a routine for setting up camp, and all went smoothly. Then, their tasks finished, they gathered around Jared for further instructions.

Libby had learned not to let his brusque manner bother her. After all, he spoke to all of them in that same clipped tone. There was no reason for her to take exception to it.

She did have to control her facial expression when Jared said, "Libby, come with me." He'd been avoiding her just as much as she'd been avoiding him. Since the afternoon he had warned her away from his men, nothing but the most polite and empty words had passed between them. He gave her instructions, but he seldom met her eyes.

And during their morning and evening swims he kept his distance. Sometimes he waited till she and the others had left the river before he went in. Perhaps the sight of her in her wet *kain* disturbed him, or perhaps he just wanted to have some time to himself. Now, following him up the trail, she wondered what had made him change his mind. She had to follow behind him. The thickly overgrown jungle brush made walking beside him impossible, and the vines called "wait-a-minute" would catch at anything that brushed them, sinking their spines into clothes and skin alike.

Though she should have been watching where she was going, she couldn't keep her eyes off his back. He swung the machete with effortless ease, and she saw

112

the ripple of muscles beneath his damp shirt. With a little smile she gave thanks that she didn't have to cut trail.

Jared made the same half-grunting, half-singing sounds that issued from the throats of Njo and Kustarto when they cut trail, the sounds that she had come to recognize as warnings to the denizens of the rain forest that man was coming through.

A sudden noise—whimpering, whispering, yet shrill—issued from the dense tangle of undergrowth to their right. It sounded unlike anything Libby had ever heard. A strange sound—something between the squeak of a little pig and the whine of a big dog. Her eyes went to Jared, and the next thing she knew she'd caught the toe of her boot in a banyan root and fallen to her knees. She did not scream or call out, but the fall brought a quick "Oh!" of surprise that she couldn't completely stifle.

The undergrowth to her right swayed and shook, and from it came a series of angry sounds. Jared was at her side instantly, jerking her to her feet with a force that made her want to cry out in pain. But she saw the warning in his eyes and sank her teeth into her bottom lip.

The noises grew louder and there, between tangled lianas and creepers, a hairy head thrust into view. Behind a curved horn two wicked little eyes stared into Libby's as the front part of the rhino came into sight. Jared's fingers tightened warningly on her arm, but she had no intention of moving. It was clear to her that the rhino was faster than either of them. If he decided to charge, there was no way to escape him.

The beast continued to survey them, the hairy snout bearing that wicked horn cocked to one side as though he were trying to make up his mind what to do.

Libby's thoughts raced. If the rhino charged, Jared would take over. But would he jump in front of her, swinging the machete? Would he push her down to the earth? Or shove her away and expect her to run? She tried to hold herself in readiness for whatever might happen.

And the rhino continued to stare. He was one of the hairy kind she'd read about. And he was small— smaller than most rhinos. But that didn't decrease the danger. For his small size made him very nimble. And she didn't need to remember that this species of rhino was renowned for ill temper. That was very clear from the animal's stance.

The rain forest seemed suddenly very silent. For a moment there was nothing but the sound of their breathing mingled with the rhino's noise. Then the background sounds began again.

Jared's fingers bit deeply into her arm. Her knee stung where it had struck a root when she fell. Sweat trickled down the valley between her breasts, tickling her damp skin. Her heart pounded so loudly that she wondered that the rhino didn't hear it and charge. And still nothing happened.

They might have been frozen into a picture frame, Libby thought, wondering how much longer this could last.

The rhino half whistled, half whimpered again and shook its head free of entangling creepers. Then, just as rapidly as they had appeared, its head and shoulders vanished. Jared's hand kept her immobile while the noise of the beast's departure faded into the distance.

She had heard no more sounds for several minutes when he finally released her arm. "Are you all right?" he asked, and she saw concern in his eyes.

"Of course." Libby didn't think it necessary to tell him that now that the danger was past her knees were shaking.

"Mean-looking customer, wasn't he?"

Libby nodded. "I guess they're not much afraid of people."

"Not at all," he said grimly. "Lucky he didn't decide to come this way." His eyes surveyed the matted jungle growth around them. "Not much room to run here."

She grimaced. Her heart was pounding in her throat, but she didn't know if it was from fear of the rhino or because Jared had been touching her. It had been weeks now since that night he had taken her so silently in the darkness. Weeks. And every day he was there before her eyes. So strong, so virile. And so distant from her, she thought, as she searched for some expression in his eyes. But they were guarded. Whatever he was thinking, Jared had no intention of letting her know. Even now, when she knew very well that he had been prepared to fight that rhino, and that he had been prepared to defend her, his eyes remained opaque.

She'd been frightened, of course. Only a fool wouldn't have been. But now she was recovered and she stood, waiting for his decision as to what they would do next.

He stood silently for a minute, as though thinking

through something. Then, with an annoyed look, he wiped the back of his hand on his khakis and turned again to cut trail. It was only then that she saw the blood. He had scraped the back of his hand, probably when he'd turned to help her up.

From the brief glimpse she had had of it, Libby didn't think it was cut deeply. But any breaking of the skin, any scrape or bruise, was dangerous out here. Because of the heat and humidity, infection could set in very quickly. Jared had to go back to camp and get antiseptic on that scrape. Immediately.

"Jared." It was the first time since they'd left Balikpapan that she'd called him anything but boss.

She saw him stiffen, then stop and turn partway to face her. "What do you want?"

Licking lips that had suddenly gone dry, she forced herself to speak. "You've got to get some antiseptic on that hand."

He shrugged, his face impassive. "It'll keep. Come on."

"Jared! I'm not going anywhere until you get that taken care of." She was suddenly enveloped in the memory of how she had massaged his tired body in those long-ago years, examining every little mark or bruise and kissing it. She wanted to reach out and touch him, so great was that welling of tenderness.

Something flickered in his eyes, flickered and was quickly gone. Could he have seen the tenderness in hers? "It's just a scrape," he said. "I'll survive. Now, if you're through playing nursemaid—"

With difficulty Libby kept calm. He was goading her, she knew. But why was he being so careless about this injury?

"I'm not *playing* anything," she said evenly. "And I'm not going anywhere until we get that scrape taken care of. You know it's dangerous to ignore the smallest injury out here. What would Tim and Nick think if they knew you were behaving like this?"

She noted the hard jutting of his jaw and searched her mind for more convincing arguments. But she had already used her best shot. If he couldn't be persuaded by considering his crew . . . "You're certainly not setting a good example."

With a muffled curse he turned completely and motioned with the machete. "All right, all right. We'll go back." Disgust reverberated in his voice. "You needn't be so concerned about my health. Nick or Tim could run this show," he said as he brushed past her.

The path he had cleared was narrow, only wide enough for one. Even though he tried to avoid her, his sleeve brushed her shoulder. The contact was slight but electric. Libby dug her nails into her palms to keep from reaching out to him. He was so hurt and bitter. She longed to throw herself into his arms, to kiss away his anger as she had done so often in their youth. But making love would not disperse this anger, this bitterness. Jared's hurt was so deep that she didn't know if it could ever be eradicated.

Finally they reached the clearing. Tim looked up from where he was cleaning fish and then, seeing Jared's stormy face, looked immediately away and kept silent. Libby hurried to find the first-aid kit while Jared threw himself down on a log and glared at the jungle.

"We saw a rhino," Libby explained to Tim as she

crossed to Jared's side and opened the antiseptic. "The boss scraped his hand."

One of Tim's grizzled eyebrows went up. "Did you tangle with him?"

"No!" Jared must have realized how testy he sounded, for his next words were more moderately spoken. "It looked pretty chancy for a while, but he finally decided we weren't worth the effort. I scraped my hand on a tree trunk."

Now, thought Libby as she knelt before him with the antiseptic, now he would blame her. If she'd just been watching where she was going—

But Jared said no more. He didn't try to take the antiseptic from her either, rather to her surprise. He just stared out into the jungle as she gently cleaned the wound.

His hand was warm in hers and, although she concentrated only on cleaning the scrape, the touch of him was making her knees weak. How could Tim, how could *anyone*, not see the way things were between her and Jared, not see how much they wanted each other?

Her hands worked gently over his torn skin. The antiseptic burned, she knew, but his hand remained rock steady.

Carefully she covered the area with clean gauze, then wrapped more around his hand to hold it. She was lingering over the task, she knew. She was doing that deliberately. If only she could make him remember some of the good parts. It hadn't been all bad, their brief marriage. There had been love and caring, too.

But finally she finished the task and got to her feet.

"Thank you, Libby." His voice was soft, almost tender, and meant for her ears alone.

She felt the red rising to her cheeks, hope beating in her breast, and she dared not look into his eyes. Her whispered reply was as soft as his. "You're welcome, Jared."

She busied herself with putting the antiseptic away and straightening things in the box until her cheeks felt cooler. Then she returned the medicine kit to its place and moved to Tim's side.

"I'm really getting to like fish," she said.

Tim chuckled. "I could always go croc hunting if you'd like a change of pace."

Libby's laugh was genuine. She knew she was pulling her weight, knew that this was just Tim's idea of a family joke. "No thanks. I'll stick to fish."

Njo and Kustarto came into the clearing then, carrying more fish to be cleaned, and Libby took a seat beside Tim and began to help.

Later that night Libby lay thinking in the darkness. She wished she'd had the nerve to ask Jared for a look at his hand again. He'd been unusually quiet all evening, and she wondered if it was hurting him. He would never say so, of course. Unlike most of the men she knew, Jared kept his pain to himself. She supposed that was because he'd been on his own at such an early age.

She twisted restlessly, and the *kain* she habitually used for a covering now moved with her. She wondered if Jared had noticed that it was the *kain* he had given her that she used to cover herself at night.

He never seemed to look directly at her. Until today.

119

What kind of job had he had in mind for her? Why had he told her to follow him into the jungle? She had no way of knowing.

A sound came out of the darkness nearby, and under the *kain* her naked body stiffened. The sound came from the direction of Jared's sleeping place, but she couldn't be sure. He no longer slept between her and the others as he had that first night. Now they slept more or less in a row. On her right lay Njo, to her left Tim, then Nick, then Kustarto, and finally Jared. Even in his sleep he kept away from her, she thought sadly.

But someone was clearly moving around. And that someone wasn't being careful, either. Libby raised herself on one elbow and squinted into the darkness. She could barely make out the shape of a man bending over the fire. Then the embers flared into flame, and she knew it was Jared. In the flickering light, wearing only his *kain,* he looked as savage and primitive as the jungle around him.

He put more wood on the fire and sank down on a log, his back to her, staring into the flames. Was he in pain? she wondered, considering if she should go to him.

Sometimes during their marriage she had awakened to find his spot in the bed vacant and had been overcome by a great wave of loss. Then she would get up to search for him, unable to go back to sleep until he was there beside her.

Did he ever remember things like that? There had been good things in their marriage—many good things. If only he would remember them as she did.

Jared moved slightly, his figure outlined against the

flames, and Libby made a sudden decision. At least she could tell him that she regretted her mistakes. Thrusting aside the mosquito net, she pulled the *kain* around her and got to her feet. Then, before she could lose her nerve, she padded on bare feet to join him.

He looked up as she appeared beside him and began to get up. "Jared, please," she whispered, laying a restraining hand on his arm without thinking.

He sank back onto his log, but his face didn't soften, and he pulled his arm away from her hand. "What do you want?" He, too, kept his voice low.

She settled down beside him, pulling the *kain* over her knees. For a long moment there was silence between them. Jared kept staring into the fire, ignoring her, and she felt her courage sinking. But she had to do this, she told herself.

"Jared, I just want to tell you—I'm sorry."

"Anyone could have tripped over a root," he said gruffly, not turning to look at her.

For a moment she didn't understand, then she realized what he was thinking. "No, Jared. I'm not talking about this afternoon."

"Well, I told you repeatedly not to come along." He kept his voice low, but it was easy to hear the anger in it.

"I'm not sorry about that either," she explained patiently. "This is my job."

There was no reply to that; she had expected none.

"Is your hand bothering you?" she asked, trying to keep her voice even. "Is that why you can't sleep?"

"No." The word was short and clipped. Silence stretched between them again.

"I thought—since you were sitting here—"

"No. The hand's fine." His voice had softened a little.

"That's good." She felt stupid. During the whole of their conversation Jared had not even turned to look at her. Nor had she looked at him. All their remarks had been directed at the fire.

She was being silly, she told herself. She'd come out here with a purpose. "I'm sorry, Jared." She made herself turn and look at him. The fire cast strange shadows over his dark face. His jaw was jutting forward at an angle that told her he was not as calm as he looked.

"I'm sorry for the mess I made of our marriage." For a moment he didn't move, then he turned slowly and stared at her. His eyes were not clouded now, she thought dimly, they burned with pain.

"You admit it?"

She made herself go on. "I know a lot of it was my fault. I—I was too young. I was just a child really."

"I guess I wasn't much better," he murmured almost inaudibly.

She hurried on. "I—I can understand why you lost patience with me. Why you—might have—wanted someone else. Why you—left me."

She saw him fighting some inner emotion, but he didn't speak.

"I'm sorry, Jared, really sorry. That was years ago. It's over now. But what was between us—"

Her hand reached out to touch his bare arm. She felt the fine hair, the firm flesh and muscle beneath her fingertips, and she leaned toward him. "What we had, Jared, it's still alive. It's there between us. Surely that means something." She felt the rising tears. "Doesn't it?"

His eyes bored into hers. He seemed about to pull her into his arms. Then he shook his head. "Passion isn't enough, Libby. We found that out seven years ago."

The sorrow in his eyes was so intense she winced. "Jared, you don't understand!" She tried to keep her voice low. "I've changed. My parents don't run my life anymore. I—I don't have any connection with my father now. Or my mother either. I—I broke with them while I was in school. They didn't approve of my major."

He shook his head. "Sorry, Libby. But it's a little too late to go back and start patching things up between us now. We're attracted to each other, yes. But that's all we have—maybe it's all we ever had."

"There was something more to it than just physical attraction, Jared," she replied softly. "There was love. If you don't remember that, if you don't remember our love—" She turned away, her voice breaking.

"Call it what you will," he said, his voice suddenly hard. "Doesn't seem to me that love would have died so easy."

"Maybe it didn't." Her whispered words were soft, and since she was turned away she couldn't tell if he had heard her. There was no reply, and she swallowed over the lump in her throat and turned to face him.

"I want you, Libby," he said in a voice husky with longing. His hand reached out to grab hers. "I make no secret of that fact. And I know you want me. Why do you need sweet, lying words? Why not face facts?"

The lump in her throat was so big she couldn't speak over it. She could only stare at him.

"You want me to lie to you. To say 'I love you.'" He shook his head. "I can't. I gave you those words once and you threw them back in my face. I won't give them to you again." His tone was low and intense. The words were firm, but not intentionally hurtful. Yet for Libby they were like the stabbing of a knife. Would she never be able to convince him that she was worthy of his trust?

Libby pulled her hand away. She felt no desire now. Jared's refusal to believe in their love tore at her heart. "There's no use talking to you," she murmured. "You don't understand anything I say."

She started to get to her feet, but one hand grabbed her bare shoulder and the other caught her chin and tilted it, forcing her to meet his eyes. "Maybe I'll never understand you, Libby," he said, his eyes unreadable. "I don't know anymore."

She tried to turn her face away, but his hard fingers kept her chin immobile.

"I'll say one thing for you, though. You've got guts. It wasn't easy for you to say what you did earlier about our marriage. You weren't the only one at fault, you know," he admitted softly. "I'll take my share of the blame. I shouldn't have gone to the new field without you." His mouth twisted. "I wanted to keep you safe. I suppose that was a mistake."

He let go of her chin, but she continued to face him for a moment longer. The look in his eyes was contemplative, as though he were gazing into the past, replaying the events that had led to their separation. She couldn't bear to see the expression of pain that flashed across his handsome features. She removed his hand from her shoulder and got to her feet. "Good night, boss."

The word put immediate distance between them. When he didn't respond, she turned and made her way back to her solitary sleeping place. And there, as she lay on her back, naked beneath her *kain*, the tears ran silently down her cheeks. Was there no way to erase the past? No way to recapture their love and make time stand still?

9

~~~~~~~~~~~~~~~~~

They made the next portage successfully, and again Libby managed her share. She felt good about that and about the work she was doing. Jared had not brought up the subject of their marriage again, but he no longer treated her more harshly than he did the men. At last, she was an accepted member of the team.

And then the rain began. "Belare, thunder god, ride storm cloud," Njo said.

They had had rains before, of course. There was always rain in these latitudes—swift, drenching downpours that dumped buckets of water and were gone.

But this rain was different. It came with sudden swiftness and it poured buckets, but then it just stayed, pouring on and on.

It rained for hours on end, rained until Jared turned and handed Libby a leather pail, motioning to the bottom of the *longbot*. She accepted the pail wordlessly—the thunder and sound of the rain made it difficult to speak—and set to her task. Kneeling there in the water, her hair and clothes completely soaked, she began to bail. Time after time she lifted and poured, and still the rain continued.

Water ran down into her eyes as she worked, and Libby felt that she was making no headway. The bottom of the canoe seemed always to be holding just as much water. The pail slipped in her wet fingers, and she banged her knuckles painfully against the side of the boat. This was crazy, she thought as she stifled a cry. It was raining so hard she couldn't even see what she was doing. How could Jared tell where they were going?

She ventured a look up at him. He was sitting erect, his eyes on the rising river. As she watched, he signaled with his hand to the watchful Njo. Bending to her task again, she saw a great root being swept past them. Her heart rose up in her throat. If that root had hit the boat, they would all be floundering in the river by now.

She risked one more look at Jared and then went back to bailing. There was no use remonstrating with him, even if she could have left her job to speak to him. Clearly he was in command. Gritting her teeth, she forced herself to bail.

Her knees felt raw from kneeling in the water, and

her shoulders ached, but still she continued to bail. She was going to do her duty if it killed her, she thought grimly. Her heart skipped a beat as she had a sudden clear picture of the *longbot,* crushed and battered, overturned in the river. But it was not herself she saw helpless in the water. It was Jared.

She shook her head. He would laugh at her for such thoughts. Jared was a survivor. He would never die in a tropical river; he would make sure of that.

Now she was being melodramatic, she told herself. None of them was going to die. Jared would protect them. Sooner or later they would have to stop. Then she would rest. But until they did, she would continue to bail, no matter how tired she got. For if her life didn't depend on it—and for all she knew it might— her reputation in Jared's eyes did. Somehow she convinced her numbed mind and aching body that if only she could keep up the bailing, Jared would finally see that she had changed.

She had no idea how long she bailed. She was one huge ache, kneeling there with the rain streaming off her. "Libby." She heard her name dimly, but she couldn't be sure. "Libby, you can stop now." Jared's strong hands took the pail from her. His hands under her armpits lifted her to her feet. She swayed clumsily. Shouldn't stand up in the boat, her hazy mind cried. And then, through the rain, she saw Njo step out of the boat. They had pulled into shore, and she hadn't even noticed. She took the hand the Dayak extended to her and managed to step ashore after him. Her knees were weak, her legs wobbly, but she stayed erect while Jared and Njo lifted the *longbot* out of the water.

"Follow Njo," Jared said. "The river's rising. We've got to go inland."

Libby nodded and set off after Njo, forcing herself to put one foot doggedly after the other. She was wet clear through, so wet that she could hardly remember what it was like to be dry. And it seemed as though every muscle in her body ached madly.

She was vaguely aware that the land was rising. How high would the river go? she wondered. How far inland would they have to walk to be safe?

By the time Njo decided to stop, she had lost even the desire to know these things. She only wanted to stop, to lie down somewhere—anywhere, even in a mud puddle—and not move. Maybe not move ever again.

That was not possible, of course. When they had followed the trail Njo hacked out for them to an area he considered safe, there was still camp to set up. And she moved with the rest of them, carrying the bamboo poles the men cut and holding them while the guides used the pliant creepers to lash them together.

Even in her exhausted state Libby marveled as the shelter took shape. They lashed bamboo between some standing trees, then covered the rough structure with a sheet of lightweight plastic. More bamboo poles were crossed at the back and sides and used to support the cut brush that was piled against them to finish the improvised shelter. The front was left open, since the slant of the roof made the water run off at the back.

Finally everything was in order, and Jared motioned to her to carry her pack inside. Numbly Libby picked it up. When she put it where he had indicated, she sank down beside it.

She realized that Tim would soon be passing out rations, but she couldn't seem to move. It didn't really matter, she thought with wry humor, she was too tired to eat anyway. She considered lying down, but getting her bag out of its waterproof covering and finding her *kain* seemed too much trouble. She would just sit for a while longer.

"Libby." It was Nick's voice. She raised her head and tried to focus on his face. He looked tired, too.

"Libby, you'd better get out of those wet clothes."

She shook her head. "Later."

"Now!" This was Jared's firm tone of command, and it jerked her head toward him. "Where's one of your *kains?* We'll hang one for a curtain and you can wear the other."

She dared not protest with Jared looking at her like that, and she forced herself to unbuckle the knapsack, to bring out one of the flowered lengths of material. He took it from her outstretched hand.

"Come on, Nick. This'll just take a minute."

Nick sent her one glance of sympathy before he followed Jared to the corner.

It was a matter of only a few minutes to stretch the gaily colored length across one corner where it made a cozy little dressing room.

Jared turned to where Libby still sat. "Use this side to get in and out," he said gently. "You can hang it on this branch." He demonstrated. "Now get out of those wet clothes. And that's an order."

The rest, short though it had been, had helped, and

Libby was able to answer, "Yes, boss." She got to her feet and retreated behind the curtain.

"If you'll just turn your back"—Jared's voice held the merest hint of amusement—"we'll change too."

She turned quickly, concealing the red that stained her cheeks. "Of course. Let me know when you've finished."

As her tired fingers fumbled with the buttons on her shirt, Libby asked herself why she was going through all this. Was there really any chance that Jared would recognize the change in her? Or was she doing all this for nothing? Wasting her time?

Nothing is ever wasted, her tired mind told her. She had learned from their marriage, and she was learning from this trip. She might not like the outcome; most of the time it seemed as though Jared would never forgive her. But she had done what she could. She had asked for forgiveness. She had behaved maturely, shouldering her share of the blame. She was carrying her part of the work, too. And all of this had been good for her, had been part of the learning experience.

She peeled off her wet shirt and bra and then realized that her pants wouldn't go down over her boots. The wet laces wanted to knot under her tired fingers, but she finally managed to get them undone, to get her boots and socks off. She wiggled her toes. They were cramped and itchy.

Then she pulled down her pants and underwear. For a moment she savored the feel of the air on her bare skin. Then she took the spare *kain* from the branch where she had hung it and wrapped it around her, tucking it in securely. She was getting used to it now. It was really a very comfortable article of clothing, she thought, as she picked up her sodden things and hung them on convenient branches to dry.

She was about to turn when she realized that the men were still changing. "Okay, Libby. We're done." It was Nick who had spoken.

She turned to see that he was wearing his cutoffs. Jared had donned his *kain*. Tim had removed his soaked shirt and put on a pair of dry trousers. The guides were nowhere to be seen.

"Njo went to cut some brush for a cooking lean-to," Tim said. "Soon as we get a fire going we'll have some coffee."

Libby unhooked the *kain* curtain and stepped out. "Sounds good."

Nick nodded. "Sounds great." He moved closer, and, though his glance was only friendly, she saw admiration in his eyes. "Kustarto went to catch some fish. If he can. The rain makes it difficult."

Libby nodded. "Does it rain like this often?" she asked as Nick helped her spread out her bag.

Nick shrugged. "It's the rainy season now." He laughed. "That means that it's slightly wetter than the dry season, which is actually very wet, wetter than anything we have in the States. But to answer your question—yes. It does rain like this often."

"Then what do we do?"

"If we're smart"—It was Jared talking again—"we rest up and sleep. Get our stuff in order. Then, when it lets up, we move on."

"How long does that usually take? For it to let up?"

Jared's glance was expressionless. "We might have

to wait two or three days for the river to go down. That's why I wanted to get here. When it quits raining, we can go ahead with our work."

Libby nodded. Two or three days. And if it continued to rain she would be cooped up in this shelter with the men. She stifled a sigh. It was hard acting normal with Jared around the other men. Her longing for him was so hard to disguise. But maybe—hopefully—they would be too exhausted to notice the way she couldn't keep her eyes off him. The way she trembled when he came near.

"We'll have some rations, then sleep," Jared said. "It'll be dark soon. Maybe the rain will let up tomorrow."

As he turned away Libby's eyes met Nick's, and the smile she saw there was warming. She returned it briefly, then finished smoothing out her bag. She certainly didn't plan to argue about sleeping. There was nothing that appealed to her more at the moment than a good *long* night's sleep.

She settled down on the bag, facing the center of the shelter. At first, sitting cross-legged had been difficult to accomplish in the *kain*, but now she was adept at it.

It was some time later that Tim materialized in front of her holding a cup of coffee. Libby accepted it gratefully. "Thanks. That'll hit the spot."

"Good old instant," Tim replied with a grin. "Fish'll be coming up. Njo got a couple already."

Libby nodded. She really didn't care for anything solid. But when the fish was cooked she would eat it. It took strength to keep up the pace Jared set. And she meant to keep it up.

There would be no relaxing dip in the river tonight, she thought as she sipped her coffee. But then, those times hadn't turned out to be much fun. It was difficult to laugh and splash with Nick when Jared was watching her every move. Sometimes it was as though she had a jailer; his eyes seemed to be always on her. She felt sure she could feel them. Yet whenever she looked at him, he was looking somewhere else. Sometimes she wished she'd taken his advice and had gone back to the States. But she only wished it for a few seconds—and only when she was feeling really tired. She'd never been a quitter, and she didn't intend to start now. Even if Jared was never able to see that she'd changed, had grown up, *she* knew it. This whole experience had been good for her. She had proved certain things to herself—proved her maturity and her ability to survive. She knew she had done her share, even if no one else was ready to admit it.

How much longer would they be? she wondered. As soon as they got back to civilization she meant to have a long shower. Being wet didn't mean being clean, especially out here in the jungle. And most especially if you had to wear Western clothes.

"Here's your fish and rice," said Nick.

"Thank you." She considered offering him a place on the bag beside her, but thought better of it. Jared would probably take exception to her doing anything like that.

She bit back a sigh as Nick moved on. Didn't Jared realize how hard he was being on her? A person needed friends. And he wasn't allowing her to develop any but the most superficial relationships.

134

That wouldn't have mattered quite so much if *he* had been her friend—or lover, her mind said. But he never talked to her about anything but the job.

Dutifully Libby ate. She wasn't hungry, and the food was not particularly flavorful, but that didn't really matter. As she forced herself to chew she had one thought in mind. When she was through eating, she would be able to sleep. Jared had said so. And maybe when she woke in the morning the rain would have stopped.

It didn't take any of them long to finish their meal. Libby was draining her coffee cup as Jared rose and stretched. "Okay, let's turn in as soon as possible. Hopefully the weather will be better tomorrow."

Libby got to her feet and began to collect the plates and cups. Jared had not relegated any kitchen tasks to her. That seemed to be Tim's province. But, like the rest of them, she did what she could, from cleaning fish to collecting dirty dishes.

Tim took them from her with a smile. "Thanks."

Libby gazed out at the steadily falling rain, then to the cooking lean-to that the guides had made opposite them. "Can I help with anything else?" she asked.

Tim shook his head. "Nope. I'll finish up." He lowered his voice. "I seen you bailing today." Both his tone and his expression indicated that he didn't think much of giving such a job to a woman. His next words confirmed it. "Didn't seem right somehow."

Libby shrugged. "It had to be done, Tim. The boss was busy and so was Njo. That just left me."

Tim frowned. "S'pose so. Anyhow, I'm gonna clean up here. You get some sleep."

She nodded. As she turned to go to her sleeping bag, Jared called to her. "Libby, come here a minute."

Her heart jumped up in her throat. Had she done something wrong?

She moved slowly across the space that separated them. "Yes, boss?"

"I want to see your hands." She couldn't tell anything from his voice. If anything, it was kinder than usual.

"They're okay." She was reluctant to have him touch her, to reawaken the desire she was trying so hard to put to sleep.

"I want to see them," he repeated gently. "Sit down."

She was forced to take a place on his sleeping bag and let him take her hands in his. He examined each one minutely. Only now did she realize that her knuckles were raw. Vaguely she remembered banging them on the side of the boat while she was bailing.

"You'll need some antiseptic on this," he said gravely. "You know how serious a break in the skin can be out here. I'm surprised you didn't report it."

She opened her mouth to protest and realized that he had her either way. If she told him she'd been too tired even to notice, he would see her as a weakling. She thought quickly. "I was just going to do that."

His eyes told her plainly that he didn't believe her, but he didn't say so. "These things can't wait, you know. Not in this climate. I thought you knew better."

"I do know, boss. Next time I'll report any injury right away."

He nodded. "Good. That's the best attitude. Sets a good example."

If she hadn't been so tired, his deliberate feeding back of the things she'd told him might have been amusing. As it was she was too tired to care.

He opened the antiseptic. "Hold still now."

Libby's hands remained rock steady as he liberally applied the biting liquid. It hurt, but she had no intention of flinching in front of him.

He examined her knuckles again. "I think I'll leave them uncovered. Be careful not to get anything in there."

"Yes, boss." She raised her eyes to his as he released her fingers. If only they were alone together, her tired mind said, she would throw herself into his arms. She didn't need lovemaking; she was too tired for that. She needed the feel of Jared's body next to hers, the good, secure feeling she had known in those long-ago nights.

But there was no security in another person. She had learned that the hard way. The only real security lay in one's self. It was not really security that she wanted from Jared now, she thought. It was love and sharing. And these he was unable—or unwilling—to give her.

His hands had been warm and steady on hers, treating her with gentleness. And was that gentleness in his eyes? Tenderness? Caring? But no, it was no more than he'd do for any one of the crew.

Without another word she got to her feet and made her way back to her bag. She knew that his eyes followed her; she could feel them boring into her back.

With a sigh she lay down, her back to them all. She would go to sleep. Jared couldn't hurt her in her sleep.

That was faulty reasoning, of course, for when she finally managed to doze off it was to find herself in a nightmare world where Jared's face was hard and cruel, where he mocked her with a parade of women, all of whom he had slept with. And then—

In her dream she called out to him. Suddenly she was awake, held by the paralysis that follows nightmares. The shelter was dark, the only light coming from the embers of the cooking fire in the lean-to across from it.

Libby lay rigid, staring at the dark roof. Her heart was pounding in her throat. Dear God! In the dream Jared had showed her his left hand and he'd been wearing a wedding ring. Then he'd motioned, and out of the shadows had come a woman—an innocent, demure young woman in bridal white. "My wife," Jared had said. "My innocent young wife."

Libby took a deep breath, tried to let out some of the tension coiled in her body. What a horrible dream. She'd been innocent when she came to Jared. He was the only man she'd ever known. But he wouldn't believe that.

She concentrated on her breathing. In. Out. In. Out. Let the tension go. In. Out. Slowly. Steadily. It was just a nightmare. Nothing more. Jared wasn't going to marry anyone. And most especially not an innocent young girl. He stayed away from such girls now. Nick had told her that. So had Jared himself.

Gradually the tension oozed out of her body. She could move her arms and legs. She stretched slowly, easily, willing her muscles to relax. It was still night. She needed her rest.

She rolled onto her side, facing the center of the shelter. A mound beside her indicated a sleeping body. But whose? When she'd gone to sleep everyone else had still been up.

In the darkness she stared at the shape beside her. It was not one of the guides; they slept by preference without bags. Was it Tim or Nick who lay there? Or was it Jared? She couldn't tell.

She listened intently. The rain outside had slowed. She could just make out the sound of breathing, steady and even. As she listened to the rhythm of it, her heart began to pound. Unsteadily she raised herself on one elbow and squinted toward him. There were less than eight inches between them. The shelter was not that big, after all, and there were six of them to squeeze into it.

Suddenly the man beside her moved. Libby dropped back onto her bag as he turned on his back. She could see better now and realized that before he'd been facing away from her.

It was Jared. She could make out the *kain* that covered his hips. She sucked in her breath, conscious of the pull of her own *kain* across her breasts. He was so close. She could easily reach out and touch him.

She bit her bottom lip. This was madness. If she did something like that, he would only scorn her. A bitter smile twisted her face. To him it would only be further evidence of the physical attraction between them, not a sign of love.

She turned onto her back, the tears rising to her

eyes. Why couldn't Jared understand? Why couldn't he see that she had changed? That she wasn't a spoiled brat any longer?

The tears trickled down her cheeks, and she raised her hands to knuckle them away, forgetting the raw spots. The salty liquid bit into the sore places and, unprepared for it, she gasped.

Had she wakened him? she wondered, lying completely still. She hoped not. Getting back to sleep would be next to impossible if she knew he was lying there awake.

But Jared didn't stir. His steady breathing continued. Rolling onto her side away from him, Libby got her legs twisted in the *kain*. Silently she untucked it and lifted her hips. She would have to use it as she normally did, as a cover. She had to sleep. She arranged it carefully over her, then forced herself to use her relaxation techniques.

Sleep returned to her eventually, and this time it was peaceful, not haunted by nightmares. It was a sudden sound that wakened her. She knew that as she opened her eyes, but she couldn't remember what kind of sound it had been. She lay quietly in the darkness, listening. There was nothing. Not even the sound of the rain.

Lifting the *kain* slightly, she rolled onto her back and then over to her other side. As she reached that position she almost cried out. Jared's hand was lying on her sleeping bag and her breast had come to rest against it. Her heart pounded in her throat. She should move away from that hand. But she didn't.

He couldn't accuse her of having done anything,

she thought grimly. It was *his* hand and it was on *her* bag. The responsibility was all his.

His fingers didn't move. They were completely relaxed. Her mind went backward in time. To the wonderful nights when they were first married. To the times when, even in sleep, they had to touch each other. How good those days had been, she thought drowsily. How good she had felt loving Jared, knowing Jared loved her. It could be that way again. She knew it could. And she drifted off once more. Into a sleep where Jared loved her, where Jared held her close and whispered that he would never let her go.

10

When Libby woke the next morning, the space beside her was empty. She was still facing toward the center of the shelter. The *kain* was tucked securely under her arms and covered her clear to her toes. Had Jared wakened with his hand still against her? she wondered. If he had, she would have liked to have seen his face. But perhaps it was just as well she hadn't. It might not have been very pleasant.

She stretched and looked around. Tim was in the lean-to stirring up some breakfast rice. Pulling the *kain* around her, Libby got to her feet. "Are they down at the river?" she asked.

Tim shook his head. "Nah. It's still too high. Kustarto found a pond. Kind of nice place. You can see the sun."

"Where is it?" Libby asked. She had grown used to the perpetual greenish light of the tropical jungle caused by the tangle of trees far above them, but the thought of swimming in a pond was intriguing.

Tim gestured with a free hand. "Kustarto cut a trail. Just stick to it."

"Have they been gone long?" she asked, releasing her braids and running her fingers through her hair.

"Not long," Tim replied.

Usually she swam with her hair up, but since they were going to be here for several days she might take this opportunity to wash it. Putting the rubber bands and hairpins in their plastic bag, she rummaged in her knapsack for her soap. One thing this trip had taught her was to be careful with her belongings. Nothing could be replaced out here, and she didn't fancy trying to tie her hair up with jungle creepers.

She set off down the trail humming a tune. She had learned that, too, she thought as she avoided a liana. In the rain forest it was wise to let the jungle creatures know you were coming.

She gazed around her with appreciative eyes. Everything was fresh and clean, a bright, vivid green that even the filtered light couldn't subdue. Wildflowers grew everywhere.

She felt very good this morning. More cheerful than she had in weeks. She was not sure why, unless it had something to do with Jared having slept beside her. In the old days he'd always claimed that touching her "recharged his batteries." Was it possible that she had gained something from him during the night? Some energy he didn't know he was giving her?

She shook her head. Whatever the reason, she felt good this morning. Her muscles were only a little stiff, and her knuckles didn't hurt at all. Their trip was almost two-thirds over. Or so Njo had estimated. And she had been a competent member of the team the whole way.

A brightly colored parrot swooped down from a branch nearby, and Libby jumped, then laughed. She hadn't bolted when they met the rhino, and she'd managed the portaging and the bailing as well as any man.

The pond was further from the camp than Libby had expected, but she took the opportunity of the walk to enjoy the beauty around her. There hadn't been much time for that. Jared set a hard pace. And his crew kept to it.

But if the river was going to take a couple days to get back to normal, they might be able to slow down a bit. She would like to have more time to enjoy the rain forest and its attractions.

The trail broadened into a clearing, and Libby stopped, enthralled. Though small, the pond was too big for the trees to meet over it. The sun reflected on the water made her squint for a moment. She glanced up once at the clear blue sky, and then her eyes went automatically to where the men were swimming.

Nick saw her first and called, "Come on in, Libby."

Jared turned then, and Libby felt his eyes on her. She put her soap on the sand and plunged into the water. It was almost cool, and it felt wonderful against her skin. She turned over on her back and floated, her hair streaming out around her.

"You look like a mermaid." Nick appeared beside her.

Libby turned her head to look at him, but remained floating. "What a lovely place."

Nick nodded. "Jared said Kustarto told him about it. That's why he insisted on pushing on yesterday."

Libby put her feet down and stood up, the water lapping around her breasts. She was no longer self-conscious about the *kain,* except when Jared stared at her with those intense eyes of his. "This is such a beautiful place." She laughed softly. "It reminds me of a Tarzan movie. I almost expect to see Johnny Weismuller and Maureen O'Sullivan come swinging out of the trees."

Nick smiled. "Some of those old movies were great. I remember seeing them on TV."

Libby nodded. "I watched them every chance I got. He was the best Tarzan."

"She was the best Jane," said Nick. "I remember him coming into their tree house and kissing her awake."

"There's one scene I'll never forget," Libby told him. "I don't remember which movie it was in. But Tarzan was on the ground, and Jane dove out of a tree and landed face down on his outstretched arms." She smiled ruefully. "For years I dreamed of a man who could catch me like that. A man I could trust like that."

"I hope you've given up such silly dreams by now." Jared's cool voice came from behind her. "Those are the fantasies of young girls. There's nothing real about

145

them. Any more than the relationship between Johnny and Maureen was real. Or even the dive that impressed you so. Some stuntwoman probably did it."

Libby turned to face him. "I don't care *who* did it. It's the symbolism that counts. Like when Superman turned back the world to save the woman he loved."

Jared snorted. "Now *that's* a daydream if I ever heard one. It's just not possible to turn back time."

He swept a hand through his wet hair. "And as for love—that's the biggest joke yet. The kind of trust you're talking about doesn't exist in real life." His laugh was brittle but she could have sworn she saw longing on his face. "Frankly, Libby, I can't see you diving out of a tree into any man's arms."

She swallowed over the lump in her throat and looked squarely into his eyes. "You're wrong, Jared. There was a man once . . . I loved him that much. I trusted him that much. I would still put my life in his hands."

For a moment he met her eyes, then he shook his head angrily. "It's all a bunch of—" He stopped, letting them supply the missing word. He glanced down at his watch. "Breakfast should be ready soon. Let's go."

Libby hesitated, then decided against washing her hair. She could do it this evening. Jared was not in the best of moods, and she didn't want to provoke him any further. Already she could feel the curiosity in Nick's glance. It would be better if he didn't start doing too much wondering about her and Jared. Jared would blame her for that, too, she thought as she followed them out of the water and scooped up her soap.

The breakfast rice was ready when they reached the camp, and Libby accepted hers silently. She'd grown used to their rather limited diet of fish and rice supplemented with jungle fruit. Of course, she could understand that it was difficult to transport a lot of supplies. And it made perfect sense to live off the land. But sometimes she couldn't help wondering if Jared might be making things unnecessarily difficult for her. It was impossible to know. And silly to spend time trying to guess.

She carried her empty tin plate and cup back to Tim and returned to her sleeping place. She looked down at the *kain* she was wearing. When they had started making camps that were to last more than one night, Jared had begun to wear his *kain* to work in as well as to sleep in. Libby had not been that brave. But this morning, with the thought of that pond still fresh in her mind, she had a notion to stay in her *kain* for work.

Jared and Nick had already moved out in the opposite direction. The Dayaks had gone down by the river to fish for supper. Tim would stay close to the camp, as always.

A small smile curved her lips as she searched out her notebooks and pen. Yes, she was going to work in her *kain*. On the spur of the moment she scooped up her soap and the bag that held her hair rubbers and pins. She would have the lovely pond all to herself, she thought happily. There would be no one to stop her from washing her hair, from swimming in the lovely jungle pool. She could do that without neglecting her work, she told herself, as she turned toward Tim.

"I'm going back to the pond," she said. "I want to take a closer look at the sand there."

Tim glanced up from the pan he was scouring. "Just don't go wandering off into the jungle."

Libby shook her head. "I give up on you, Tim. You're the biggest male chauvinist on the face of the earth." She laughed as she said it.

And he grinned as he replied. "Maybe I am. But I jest want you to be careful." His lined face twisted into a sheepish smile. "I got sort of used to having you around. Wouldn't be the same without you."

A lump rose in Libby's throat. "Thanks, Tim. I appreciate that." She turned toward the trail. "See you later."

The trail seemed familiar now, she thought, as she headed back toward the pond. The jungle greenery had lost its morning freshness, but it was still lush. On an impulse she reached out and picked a red orchid to tuck behind her ear. No one would be seeing her while she worked. If she wanted to feel soft and feminine, it was no one's business but her own.

"You Tarzan, me Jane." She murmured the words aloud and then sighed. If only Jared still loved her. How lovely it would be to play at being Tarzan and Jane here in this beautiful place.

The trail opened into the little clearing and she paused, drinking in its lush beauty. At first so much green had been overwhelming, almost stifling in its fecundity, but now she had grown to like it. She could name some of the flowers by now, the fragrant frangipani, the beautifully hued bougainvillea. And, of course, orchids were everywhere in the rain forest. Orchids in all colors: red like the one she had stuck behind her ear, yellow, white and turquoise, as well as the more common mauve and lavender.

To one side of the pond grew a huge banyan tree, its aerial roots spreading out to create a whole little grove. Behind it she recognized the towering teak trees with their wood so hard and durable that it would last through almost anything. There were other trees in the forest, too: camphor, fig, bamboo, rattan.

The pond was quiet, its surface a smooth sheet except where the waterlilies clustered, their pink blossoms spread above large waxy leaves.

She would have liked being Jane, she thought, as she relished the unspoiled beauty of the pond. If she and Jared could have stayed here—away from the influence of other people—how idyllic their life could have been. She could see him, nothing but a loincloth around his lean hips, his skin burned brown by the tropic sun.

He would make a good Tarzan, she thought, as she moved toward the inviting water. Her hair was still loose around her shoulders, the orchid behind her ear. She would take a quick swim, then wash her hair and let it dry in the sun.

She put down her soap and walked into the clear, blue water. I'm Jane, she told herself as she rolled over and began to float. Tarzan is out in the jungle getting our breakfast. She had a quick picture of Jared swinging through the trees.

Probably Jane didn't bother with that skimpy leather thing when she swam, Libby told herself. Probably she and Tarzan, too, swam in the nude. Libby felt a flush spreading over her body. She'd never gone skinny-dipping. The part of Texas where she lived had been too populated for that kind of fun. For a minute she continued to lie there, the water supporting her. What would it feel like to be completely naked, to feel the water against all her skin? It would certainly be a sensuous experience. And this was the perfect place for it. The perfect time. Everyone was away at their various tasks. They would be gone for several hours at least. And the pond was all hers. When would she ever have such a chance again?

Libby put her feet down and stood up. She was going to do it, she thought, her eyes sparkling with a sense of daring. She was going to take off her *kain* and swim in the buff. She was going to do it now—before she lost her nerve.

The water lapped around her knees as she unwound the *kain* and wrung it out before draping it over a nearby branch. Then she turned and slipped back into the water, reveling in the feel of it against her naked skin.

She moved slowly, swimming with long, languorous strokes. Her body tingled from the unexpected feel of the water. How wonderful to live in this magnificent setting. With a sigh she rolled over onto her back. Keeping her eyes half-closed against the sun's brightness, she floated in lazy contentment, the fragrance of the lotus lilies in her nostrils.

This was paradise. This peace and beauty. Or it could be if only Jared would share it with her. She let her eyes close completely.

If they were really Tarzan and Jane, Jared would be coming soon. And seeing her floating here like this he would slip noiselessly into the water and join her. They would swim and dive, cavorting like children. He would pull her under the water and kiss her, their bodies intertwining in the green depths. They would play in the pond like innocent water creatures until he carried her, breathless with joy, up onto the sandy bank and there consummated their love.

A soft smile curved Libby's lips. It was a beautiful fantasy. And though there had been no real Tarzan and Jane, surely their story had enriched the lives of hundreds of thousands of people. Their story—and the example of their love. Jared was wrong to think that such love was an illusion. It did exist. It had existed for them. She knew that. It would exist still if she hadn't killed it.

Sudden tears rose behind her closed eyelids. She loved him so much. Why couldn't he return that love?

She was being silly, she told herself sternly. She had work to do. The real Jared would throw a fit if he knew she was goofing off like this. She'd better get out of here and get busy.

But the water was so comfortable, so relaxing. And it was good to be alone. Sometimes now she felt that she never had a minute to herself.

Something slid slowly across her bare flank. A fish, thought Libby. She'd been swimming in jungle waters too long to be frightened by the touch of some small water creature. She inhaled deeply; the fragrance of the lilies was heavy in her nostrils. In another minute she would get to work.

Something moved now against her side and it was not a casual movement. It felt—Libby's eyes flew open—it felt like a hand! As she blinked against the brightness of the sun, the hand—for that's what it was—moved down across her bare stomach.

Her head turned automatically to the side from which the hand came, but she knew somehow, even before her eyes met his, that it was Jared whose hand had caressed her.

For a minute her numbed mind refused to work. Finding him there was so like her fantasy that before she quite knew what had happened she had smiled at him invitingly and slowly sunk below the water. He was naked, too, she saw as she opened her eyes in the underwater dimness. And she ran a hand up his strong leg.

Then he was underwater with her and, just as in her fantasy, their naked bodies intertwined. She felt the long, lean length of him as his lips brushed hers. Then he motioned to her to follow him. In a silent underwater ballet they moved through the dimness. He was all grace and flow, but so strong, so male. And behind him, repeating his movements, she was all female.

This couldn't be really happening. It was all a part of her fantasy. Maybe she'd fallen asleep floating there near the lilies. Maybe all this was a lovely dream. As he glided up toward the surface she was right behind him. In that brief moment when she had smiled at him, she'd seen the longing in his eyes. Longing and need. He'd looked so like the old Jared then.

He surfaced and shook the wet hair from his eyes. Libby did the same. She searched her mind for something to say, something that wouldn't break the beautiful spell that enclosed them.

The water came to his hips when he put his feet on the sandy bottom. It lapped gently around her waist as she stood facing him. She sought his eyes. The longing was still there. Longing—and tenderness. "Jared—"

His finger across her lips silenced her. "Me Tarzan, you Jane," he whispered as his hand moved from her mouth down across her chin and throat to her breast. "No talk."

Her flesh quivered under his touch. She needed him. These last weeks had been hellish, being so close to him all the time and having him treat her like a stranger.

His finger circled her breast, tracing the rosy areola. Then he went to his knees and kissed it, his lips sending waves of desire through her. Libby shivered with delight as, steady and sure, his hands encircled her waist and pulled her down to him.

On their knees there in the water he clasped her to him. All her senses seemed heightened by the water that surrounded them. It lapped gently at her shoulders as his arms encircled her and drew her against him. The crisp hair of his chest caressed her sensitive breasts. The longing between them was so strong that it seemed to vibrate in the air.

His lips kissed her shoulder, his tongue making a trail up her throat, over the pulse that throbbed there, to the sensitive spot behind her ear. She trembled as she rested her forehead on his hard shoulder. Then, turning her head slightly, she ran her tongue up his throat, lightly traced the lobe of his ear in the caress that had once been his very favorite. His shiver of delight told her it was still so.

Slowly, lightly, she drew her tongue across his cheek and down to his chin where she traced the curve of his jaw and then dropped her head to kiss his Adam's apple.

The arms that held her grew tighter as a deep sigh came from between his lips. Then his mouth covered hers. His lips were wet and tasted, as his ears and throat had, of the pond water. Lightly, gently, they caressed hers until they softened and opened for him. His tongue traced the sensitive inner curve of her lips, then moved on. Not exploring, for he knew every part of her body in exquisite detail. Not demanding, for she opened to him willingly. But with a certain sense of joy, as one would feel on coming home to a beloved place and finding it still as wonderful as one had remembered it.

Her hands moved from their steadying position on his shoulders as her arms encircled his neck and she yielded herself to him. For a while she remained passive, allowing him to take the initiative, but then she followed his movements, her tongue caressing the inside of his mouth. Every cell in her body was on fire with need for him and she poured that need and love into her kisses. She didn't know how her fantasy had become reality, but it had. And she was going to go with it.

When he withdrew his lips, he smiled. Then, releasing his hold on her waist, he slid onto his back, inviting her with a gesture to swim facing him. And so they moved across the pond, their bodies in perfect unison. So strong was the pull between them, the energy that their desire emanated, that the water seemed an extension of their bodies. The water that seemed to separate them really connected them.

At the edge of the circle of lotus lilies he motioned to her to smell. Up close their fragrance was deep and heady. Libby's smile was ecstatic.

The red orchid that she had worn into the water earlier had floated there and lodged against one of the huge, waxy leaves. He pulled it free and tucked it behind her ear, his fingers trailing a gentle caress down her cheek. Then he was off again, swimming toward the banyan tree where he pulled himself up by one of the thick roots.

From the water Libby watched as he climbed higher, weaving in and out among the tangled vines and creepers. When he reached one great branch that jutted out over the water, she saw what he meant to do. The branch made a natural diving board.

As his body sliced neatly into the water Libby's heart pounded. Then she paddled toward the root and pulled herself up. She wanted to dive, too.

Getting there was a little tricky, but she managed, standing finally on the same branch. She smiled at him as she dove, her naked body arching in the air before it sliced cleanly into the water.

When she opened her eyes in the greenness of that underwater world, he was there beside her, his body entwining itself with hers. It was thus, with their flesh touching, that they kicked their way to the surface. And there he rolled once more onto his back, only this time he pulled her closer. Only inches separated their bare bodies as they slowly circled the pond in rhythm until they reached the banyan tree again.

Libby grabbed at a convenient root and pulled herself up, half expecting him to follow. But when she turned, about ten feet off the ground, and looked back, he was standing still in the shallows, only his eyes following her.

She paused there on the branch above him, and it came to her—in a flash of inspiration—the perfect way to prove her love and trust in him. His eyes were still on her and she extended her arms in a catching motion, then invited him to do the same. She could see the puzzlement on his face as he copied her gesture, searching her face for the reason behind it.

She saw the realization hit him, heard his anguished, "Libby! Don't!" Then he was climbing toward her and the moment had passed. Perhaps that was not trust, she thought, that blind swoop of Jane into Tarzan's waiting arms. Perhaps trust was something else, something less dramatic. Like taking the hand that Jared was extending to her, like letting him put his arm around her. She wrapped both her arms around his neck as he held her tightly with one arm and with his other hand pulled a big creeper toward them. He yanked it twice sharply to be sure it would hold their weight, this cautious Tarzan of hers, then he stepped off the branch, swinging them both to the ground. Libby's delighted laughter pealed out into the jungle. This was the Jared she loved, the Jared who could share her fantasies, even improve on them.

When he released the creeper, he swung her up into his arms and carried her away from the tree to a sandy bank. There he went to his knees and laid her gently on the sand. For long hungry moments his eyes devoured her face. They were not closed or cloudy now, those eyes. Sheer longing burned there. And tenderness. She could not mistake that look of tenderness.

She felt the warm sand under her bare back and hips, the touch of the sun on her naked body. His breath rasped in her ear, and then he was covering her face with tantalizing little kisses. She felt the pounding of his heart against her own. His arms encircled her; his hands cradled her head while his mouth devoured hers.

There was urgency in his kiss, urgency and demand. But it did not frighten her. Her own need was clamoring. His body covered hers, and she arched up against him, suppliant, needing. Her arms went around him, her fingers digging into the hard muscles of his back. When he raised himself, she opened eagerly to him. So ablaze was she with desire that his entrance almost pushed her over the peak.

His mouth covered hers again as his body moved against her. Every part of her gloried in the feel of him.

His breath came hard and fast as his mouth crushed against hers. The burning joy spread out from her center as she reached the joyous climax of her love. But he wasn't finished, and she rode the crest of the wave, enveloped in ever-widening circles of delight until finally he collapsed against her, his own consummation complete.

They lay quietly as their breathing returned to normal. Libby wished never to have to move, never to have his body separate from hers. Everything was right now—complete.

Finally he stirred. Her arms went around him automatically, clasping him close. He relaxed again for a few minutes, and when he again began to raise himself she didn't try to stop him.

He rolled to one side and she moved automatically to lie against him. She still could not quite believe that this had happened.

"Jared?" The word was a soft whisper.

"What?" His whisper was equally soft. It was as though they both feared to break the spell of enchantment that bound them.

"I—" Now she was afraid to speak, afraid to lose this magic moment. "How did you know—"

"That you were thinking of diving out of that tree?" he interrupted. "I know *you*, Libby. You can't prove anything by a melodramatic thing like that."

His voice remained soft and she did not feel that she was being scolded. Perhaps it was because his hand was still caressing her back. "I don't know if I would have really done it."

"I couldn't take that chance."

There was a catch in his voice, and her heart leaped with hope. "Why, Jared?"

There was a long pause, and she felt his body begin to withdraw from hers. It frightened her so that she wanted to clutch at him, that first, almost imperceptible, pulling away.

"We're in the middle of the rain forest," he said gravely. "You could have been injured. Or injured me. We'd be in a hell of a fix then."

"I see," she said, swallowing over the lump in her throat. She took a deep breath. "Jared, please, couldn't you love me again? Even a little?"

She felt the stiffening of his body, but his voice

158

remained grave, and there was no anger in it. Nevertheless his words made her want to weep.

"I told you, Libby. No lying words. We're very good together. Sexually. I've always admitted that. But our marriage is dead. And love is meaningless to me now."

"But I've changed!" She moved so she could see his face. "I've grown up. Haven't I?"

He nodded. "I'll grant you that, Libby. And you've certainly done your share on this job. You've proved to me that you can handle just about anything. But that doesn't change the facts. I've told you, I no longer believe in love—or in the trust and sharing you seem to think goes with it. I just can't give you what you're asking for."

He untangled himself from her arms. "Thank you for letting me share your fantasy." His smile was grave. "I've seen my share of Tarzan movies, too." The smile faded. "But now we've got to get back to work. I'll see you later. Back at camp." He got to his feet and looked down at her. "I'd rather we kept what happened here to ourselves."

"Of course," she replied, fighting to keep back the tears.

He turned then and moved off into the water.

Raising herself on one elbow, she watched him glide across the pond, his powerful arms moving him swiftly toward the lilies. He dove under the clustered blossoms and in her mind's eye she could see him moving easily between the lily stems. Then his head appeared on the other side. With strong, steady strokes he reached the opposite bank. There he climbed ashore, picked up his discarded *kain*, gave her a brief wave and disappeared into the jungle.

Libby fell back on the sandy bank. Though the sun's rays fell directly on her, a fit of shivering overtook her, and she clasped her arms around herself. She had to think about this. How could he make love like that and *not* love her? She couldn't understand it. But the shivering stopped, and she stretched her satisfied body. He had admitted she'd changed. That was something. That was a lot! And this job wasn't over yet.

She stretched again and got to her feet. She had work to do.

11

~~~~~~~~~~~~~~~~~~

When Libby returned to the camp later in the day, she had done all she could at the pond. She would follow Jared's lead, she had decided. If he wanted to pretend that their lovemaking had not happened, she would go along with him. But she knew it *had* happened. And so did he.

As she entered the clearing, Tim was busy cleaning fish.

He looked up as she approached. "You been gone a long time," he observed, his eyes settling on her.

Libby nodded. "I had a lot to do."

"Thought maybe the boss gave you some extra work. He come back shortly after you left. Asked where you were."

Libby's heart caught in her throat. She bent, putting her things back in her pack, postponing an answer.

"There you are, Libby." Jared's voice came across the clearing. "Get out your map of this area. I want to check something on it."

"Sure, boss." She kept her voice calm. Apparently, Jared intended to act as though he had not seen her since morning. "Which one do you want?"

"The one you were working on yesterday." His voice was flat and noncommittal, and his eyes avoided hers as she crossed the space that separated them and extended the notebook to him.

"Yes, that's it."

Libby turned back to where Tim sat, picked up a knife and reached for a fish.

"Boy, what I wouldn't give for a good steak," Tim growled. "We must have et a million fish by now."

Libby laughed. "I know how you feel, but it's ice cream I dream about. A gigantic sundae covered with hot-fudge sauce, topped with whipped cream, nuts and a cherry."

Tim nodded. "I'll getcha one soon as we get back to Balikpapan. We'll go up to Kampury Amerika. They got everything from home there."

Libby nodded. "I'll take you up on that." She smiled. "As long as you don't expect me to eat croc first."

Tim shook his head. "Nah, that ain't necessary. I know lotsa guys don't like croc meat. Don't mean nothing. You got as much guts as any man. Now that I seen you in action, I'd be glad to work in the same crew with you any time."

A sudden lump filled Libby's throat. This was rare praise from the grizzled old veteran. "Thank you, Tim. I appreciate that."

Jared's laugh startled them both. "He's just pleased to have help cleaning the fish."

Tim frowned. "Nah, boss, that ain't it at all. I seen Libby work. She's as good as any man. Better 'n some." And he looked up from the fish in his hand to meet Jared's eyes.

But Jared refused the confrontation. "Have it your way," he mumbled before he disappeared again into the jungle.

For a minute Tim stared at the place where he had vanished. Then he grimaced. "I don't know what's eating that man. He's been meaner'n hell this whole trip."

"I thought he was always like that." Libby attempted a light tone, but Tim's reply was serious.

"Nah. He ain't the lovey-dovey kind, but he's allus been pretty fair tempered. Now"—he shook his head —"he's touchier than a granddaddy croc."

He threw the fish he had just cleaned into the pile with the others. "First I thought it was you. Being a woman and all. But it can't be that. You ain't done nothing wrong." He picked up another fish. "Oh, well, guess there ain't nothing we kin do about it. We'll make out okay."

Libby, scraping scales, nodded. If only she had someone to talk to, someone to give her another perspective on what had happened today. The questions chased round and round in her head as she continued to clean fish. But, as usual, there were no answers.

Nick appeared, carrying a bunch of wild, red-skinned bananas over his shoulder. "I brought dessert," he said, sending Libby a grin.

"Good." She forced a lightness into her voice that she didn't feel. "I dearly love fish and rice, but enough is enough."

Nick put the bananas down. "I prefer *pisang tuju*," he said cheerfully. "The little tiny finger-sized ones, but I suppose these'll do."

"This is a survey trip, not a gourmet's tour." Jared's voice was sharp, and they all turned to him in surprise as he reentered the clearing. For a moment the silence was heavy as each of them sought for something to say, some way to ease the tension.

It was Jared who did it. "We'll be back in civilization before long," he said finally, his voice more cordial. "Then we can all relax and enjoy ourselves."

"Yeah, boss." Tim picked up the conversation. "What're you gonna eat first, Nick? I'm fer steak. And Libby wants a hot-fudge sundae."

Nick broke off a banana and peeled it, offering it to Libby. She shook her head. "My hands are dirty." She grimaced. "Fish."

Nick smiled and extended the banana. "I'll be your hands. Have a bite."

Libby's teeth sank into the ripe fruit. By now she was used to the fact that bananas could have many nuances of flavor. She would never again think of bananas as the simple yellow fruit she'd been accustomed to. Some were sweet, some were not. Some could not be eaten raw and others had edible skins.

"Well," she teased, ignoring Jared's dark look, "what's your food fantasy?"

Nick frowned, concentrating. "I guess it's stuffed pork chops. I'm a sucker for stuffing."

Libby smiled. "Tim thinks we can find a place in Kampung Amerika."

Tim nodded. "Yeah. They got everything there." He exchanged a quick look with the others. "What about you, boss?"

Libby held her breath while her hands continued steadily at their task. Tim was offering Jared a chance to redeem himself, to make up for his previous grouchiness. That Jared recognized this she could tell from the way he regarded her.

"I guess what I'd like best is big plate of lasagna, with fresh Italian bread and butter."

Nick and Tim groaned in unison. "Wouldn't that taste great, though?"

"Yes." Libby nodded her enthusiastic agreement. "How much longer do you think we'll be?" Her eyes sought Jared's face, but his gaze revealed nothing.

"Two weeks or so," he replied. "The river seems to be going down. We'll be able to move on tomorrow or the next day. One more rapids, a couple more camps, and then we reach Longpahanghai where we radio for the copter. And that's it."

Libby added her fish to the growing pile that would be the main part of dinner. "How soon do you think they'll send in the seismograph crew?"

Jared shrugged. "Hard to say. Depends on how bad they need the oil. And a couple hundred other little things—like who's in office, and what the cartels are doing."

165

He made a face. "That's their problem. Ours are over once we hit Longpahanghai."

His eyes swept over Libby's face, then went on to Nick's. "How did things look today?"

Nick answered first. "This seems like an excellent area. Most of the signs are right."

Jared's eyes returned to Libby. She frowned. "I'm afraid I have to agree."

Jared's forehead creased, and Tim and Nick both stared at her.

"Why 'have to'?" Jared asked.

She allowed herself a rueful smile. "This jungle is so beautiful. Wild and free. I hate to think of this place—" She dropped her eyes. "Of that lovely pond—all ruined by clanking rigs and derricks, men trampling on everything. All the primitive beauty destroyed."

Jared shook his head. "There's no place in the oil business for empty-headed romanticism. If people think they need the oil that's here, they'll take it. That's the way it is." His dry smile didn't reach his eyes. "They call it progress and we're all part of bringing it to pass."

"I think I understand what Libby's saying." Nick's words were soft but determined. "There are so few really primitive places left in the world. She just hates to see one of them destroyed."

He turned his smile on her. "But I'm afraid the boss is right. The price we pay for progress has to be paid. We don't know how to stand still. Mankind must always be moving forward."

Libby raised an eyebrow. "Moving forward isn't necessarily progress," she retorted. "Especially if you're moving forward toward destruction. But I didn't mean to begin any deep philosophical discussion. It's just that I've grown to love the jungle. It has a beauty and a power all its own." She did not glance at Jared. She didn't want the others to pick up on anything.

"I wouldn't worry none about the jungle," Tim commented. "It's powerful, all right. This old rain forest's been here a long time. It'll be here a lot longer. We might trample it down a bit, but it'll come back." He grinned at Libby. "Soon as we've gone, it'll start taking over; creepers and bushes'll cover everything. In a little while no one'll be able to tell we've been here. The jungle will have reclaimed its own."

"Tim's right," said Jared. "And now this crew has work to do." He crossed the clearing and laid Libby's notebook inside the shelter. "This looks good. See you later."

The next days passed quickly for Libby. Too quickly, she thought, as they drew closer to Longpahanghai. Jared avoided her even more than he had before. She was never alone with him, and even though she spent many wakeful nights hoping, he never got up to sit by the fire again.

Time was running out. But she was not giving up.

As they set up camp one evening, Jared said, "This is our next to last night out. Day after tomorrow we reach Longpahanghai and radio for the copter." His glance swept over Libby and settled on Tim. "Then it'll be R-and-R time."

"Me, fer one, will be glad," Tim replied. "I'm gonna

sink my choppers in that there steak. And then I'm gonna get me a pretty—" He stopped suddenly, his face reddening.

Jared laughed. "It's okay, Tim. Libby's a big girl now. You can have your pretty little you-know-what. No doubt Libby'll be looking for some companionship, too."

His eyes were bright as he surveyed her, but Libby met his gaze coolly.

It was Nick who came to her defense. "I expect that by now we're all hungry for some intimate companionship. After all, we're human beings."

For a minute Jared looked as though he would reply to this, and not too pleasantly, but then he turned his attention to his food.

Unshed tears prickled in Libby's eyes, and for a few minutes she was silent, her eyes downcast. When she looked up, Nick was gazing at her with concern. She flashed him a grateful smile. "Is there a long house between here and Langpahanghai?" she asked.

Nick nodded. "I believe so. Njo should know. Why do you ask?"

"I'd like to see one up close." Her glance included Jared in her next remark. "It seems strange to have been out here all this time and never visited a long house. Do you suppose we could stop at one? Not to sleep or anything, but just for an hour or so?"

Jared's face was dark and distant, but it was almost always that way these days. "There's not much to see."

Tim laughed. "We could get the chief to show her his collection of heads."

Libby's smile told Tim she knew he was teasing.

"I thought headhunting was outlawed after World War II."

"It was," Nick replied. "But this is far into the interior. Not much government authority. The old chiefs were reluctant to bury their heads. They might have given up the practice, but they want to hold on to the ones they have. It's kind of like asking a sports pro to bury his trophies. Or even his favorite rabbit's foot. The heads weren't just heads, you know."

"I know. Njo told me. Having a man's head meant getting his courage, his power, and being able to use it yourself."

Nick nodded. "It's a rather unusual way to treat one's heroes. But of course they only took heads from outside their own tribe."

"Of course," said Jared dryly, and Libby wondered if he had ever thought of what Njo had told her—that in the old days Jared's head would have been much prized. "But to answer your question, I suppose we can stop for an hour or so tomorrow. We've finished in good time."

"Thanks." She was careful to keep her voice only casually friendly.

Jared shrugged. "You might as well get a close look at the real thing. Life in the jungle isn't much like it's painted in the movies. You might as well see that firsthand."

She knew this was meant as a reprimand. He didn't need to mention Tarzan and Jane to make his point. She forced herself to meet his eyes, to reply cheerfully. "I'm grateful to you for giving me the opportunity."

"Maybe they'll be tattooing a boy," Tim said, seemingly oblivious to any undertones in their exchange. "I seen 'em do that. Them little fellers never make a sound." He grinned. "Makes 'em look ferocious."

"I think I read somewhere that the Dayaks were the source of the 'wild men of Borneo.'" Libby was only too glad to move the conversation on.

"Yes." Inadvertently, Nick was helping her. "Kalimantan is part of what was once Borneo. The upper part—now called Sabah—is a state in Malaysia. I guess if someone like Njo was coming at you with a spear, you'd think of him as a wild man."

Libby's chuckle was genuine. "You can be sure I would."

12

~~~~~~~~~~~

The next afternoon when she stepped out of the *longbot* Libby was glad to have come in peace and friendship, glad that the brown faces surrounding her were wreathed in smiles. Bare-breasted women, babies on their hips, smiled at her, revealing the blackened teeth Njo found so attractive. Their only garment seemed to be a *kain* around the hips, and they seemed supremely unconscious of their bare breasts.

Remembering Njo's remarks about long ears, she looked for the earrings he had described. Most of the older women had elongated earlobes, some reaching almost to their shoulders because of the tremendous weight of the rings in them, but some of the younger ones seemed to have moved away from the custom, wearing only one or two rings.

But if Libby was interested in the appearance of these women, they were equally engrossed with hers. Her hair, in particular, seemed to draw them, and they pointed to it excitedly.

"They don't see many blond women around here," Nick commented. "You're something special to them. In fact, they don't see many foreigners at all."

Libby returned the smiles, wondering what these women thought of her wearing trousers. Did she seem as strangely exotic to them as they did to her?

Nick's hand was on her elbow as they followed Jared up to the long house. "That's the chief," Nick whispered as an elderly man literally covered with tattoos came to meet them. A short exchange took place between Jared and the chief.

Libby wished she could understand the language, especially when the old chief's black eyes came to rest on her.

"What're they saying?" she asked Nick.

"The chief is welcoming us, inviting us to eat. Jared's saying we will. You just take a little of each thing. For politeness's sake. And always use your right hand."

He paused and she prodded him with her elbow. "What did he say about me?"

"The chief wanted to know why he brought a woman into the jungle." Nick's smile seemed a little strained. "Wants to know who you are."

Libby's heart pounded in her throat. "And what did Jared tell him?"

"It's nothing to worry about."

"What did he say?" Libby insisted.

"He said you were taboo. That there's a curse on you and the man who touches you is doomed to fall under your spell forever."

She thought her heart would stop beating, and she knew her face paled.

"It's not important," Nick repeated. "Jared had to tell them something. And the way you two get along— or don't—he could hardly tell them you belong to him."

Libby ran her tongue over dry lips. "And what's he doing with this cursed woman?" she asked, managing to keep her voice fairly calm.

"The old chief probably thinks we've come up river to get rid of you."

"Get rid—" She couldn't go on.

"Be reasonable, Libby. No sane native would keep a cursed woman around. And he wouldn't sell her—at least not to his friends. At any rate, it's only a lie to keep you safe."

His eyes searched her face, and she saw his worry. "I wouldn't have told you if I'd thought it'd bother you. Jared's only trying to assure your safety."

She made herself nod. "I know." But inside she knew something else. Jared meant for her to know what was going on. He himself had gestured to her in a way that she couldn't have ignored. But why had he used the word "doomed"? If he didn't love her, if his feelings for her were really dead, he wouldn't have used a word like that. Would he?

Nick chuckled. "The chief has offered him the use of the medicine woman. Says maybe she can erase the spell. He says it's foolish to waste a woman."

Libby forced herself to smile. "I suppose I should be pleased."

"But Jared's telling him—" He paused and frowned.

"You might as well go on." Libby sighed.

"He's telling the chief the spell's too strong. Any man who touches you is doomed. Now they're moving on to other subjects. The condition of the river and such. The chief has invited him up on the veranda to talk."

"What about us?"

"We're free to wander around. What do you want to see?"

She watched Jared follow the aging chief up the notched log that served as a ladder. She wished to get away from him, for a while at least. "Let's look around on the ground first."

"Okay by me."

As they moved off, two small pigs came rushing out from under the long house, squealing and snorting.

Nick smiled. "All the livestock lives under the long houses, including the pigs."

"I can see." Libby followed him to where two women were pounding some kind of white substance. "That's the pith from the sago palm," Nick explained as they stopped to watch. "It takes fifteen years for a palm to mature. When it produces a flower spike, they know it's time to cut it down. They carve out the piths and make them into cakes or a kind of gruel. It hasn't

174

got much flavor, but it's a real staple in their diet. Supplements the hill rice they grow by the slash and burn method. Unfortunately, it hasn't much nutritional value either."

Libby nodded. She looked to her left. "What are those women weaving?"

Nick turned. "They're making baskets. The natural yellow of the rattan strips is decorated with red and black ornamental parts. They make conical containers to carry their belongings when they travel. Mats to sit and sleep on. Covers for their food."

Libby smiled and sidestepped a pecking hen. "The Dayaks may live in the deep jungle, but they're certainly artistic."

Nick grinned. "They haven't always lived so far inland. Years ago the arrival of the Malays drove them away from the coast. The Malays are Muslim." He laughed. "As you can see the Dayaks are very fond of pork—a dish Muslims find unclean. But this is minor stuff as far as artistry is concerned. They're excellent weavers. Njo!" He gestured to the guide who was talking to one of the village men.

"Yes, boss?"

"Ask your friend if there's anyone in the village working on an *ikat*."

"I ask." Njo spent a few minutes in conversation while a ring of curious dogs and cats, apparently resigned to living in harmony with each other, sniffed at Libby's boots.

"In long house," Njo said. "His woman show you."

"Thank you, Njo."

Libby moved off, the dogs and cats trailing along.

The notched log was easier to climb than it looked. Nick did not extend a hand to help her, and she gave him a brief smile as she reached the top.

Njo clambered quickly after them. "This *ikat*," he said, motioning to a woman who was weaving on a loom stretched out on her body.

Libby bent closer. The thread was dyed, she realized, dyed in a variety of colors.

Nick smiled at her questioning look. "The thread is dyed first. Tie-dyed. They use coconut thread to wrap it before dipping."

"It's beautiful." Libby admired the bright multicolored weaving. "What is made from it?"

Njo grinned. "*Ikat* show place of gods. Old time *ikat* hold heads."

Libby nodded. "A sacred cloth."

Njo smiled. "You like bead work." And he led her along to where another woman was making a carrying basket.

"Hold baby," Njo said proudly.

Libby smiled, admiring the lovely display of color. "Lucky baby to be carried in that."

"Men carve," Njo said. "You look chief's house. All carved. More than here."

For the first time Libby noticed the carvings around the door frames and posts, even on the railings of the veranda.

Njo stooped and picked up a bamboo container that held beads. "You look," he said, indicating the surface.

Now Libby saw that the surface was engraved. Spirals and triangles, intricate curving designs and flowing S-lines covered the small container. "It's lovely," she said, handing it back carefully.

"Men make *bukung.*" Njo made a fierce face and cupped his hands to his chin. "Have beards. Long teeth."

"Masks," Nick explained.

Njo glanced around. "Come. You see old man. Much pictures." He slapped his bare chest.

Moving around the groups of working women, Libby and Nick followed to where an old man sat in state. As they drew nearer, Libby saw that his chest, shoulders and legs were one mass of tattoos.

Njo smiled and pointed. "Here trip and trip. Here fight bad bull. Here see spirit. You look. Grandfather like."

As Libby bent to admire the tattoos the old man flashed her a smile. She returned it. "Tell him I thank him for letting me see," she told Njo.

"I tell." Njo spoke briefly to the old man, then turned to her. "He say tattoo to see." He grinned, revealing his blackened teeth. "He say long time ago he young. He see much places. No see woman have sun hair. He like."

"Thank you," Libby said to the old man.

There was a lot to be said for this society, she thought as she got to her feet. It respected age. And the arts.

"Nick! Libby!" Jared's voice came through the myriad sounds around them. "Come over to the *aminaja's* long house."

"Coming, boss." Nick turned to Libby. "He wants us."

177

"Right," she said.

As they descended from the long house and approached the chief's, Libby noted that it was higher and longer than the other. Its ridged roof was more ornately decorated. A herb garden, a mound of stones and a row of grotesque idols were situated in front of it.

"The herbs are sacred," Nick explained as they passed. "The stones are genealogical, representing the lineage and wealth of a family and its warriors. The idols are household gods."

Libby nodded and followed him up the log ladder. Bas-reliefs stood out on the veranda pillars. An ebony door to the interior showed a carved peacock on its surface. She glanced at the wood railings that enclosed the veranda. Dragons and snakes were carved there.

"Sit down, Libby," Jared said. "And keep quiet. The chief wants to look at you."

Stifling a sigh, she dropped cross-legged to the mat. It was unfair of Jared to use his position to make life difficult for her. But he was head of this crew, and it was part of her job to obey him.

The chief surveyed her for some minutes while she tried unsuccessfully to keep the blood from rising to her cheeks. She felt Nick's sympathetic look but didn't raise her eyes to his. It seemed more "womanly," she thought with sharp irony, to look down at the woven mat.

Suddenly the old man clapped his hands. The ebony door opened slowly and a wrinkled old woman appeared. She seemed weighted down with huge bronze bracelets and looked very fragile.

"The *wadian*," Nick whispered as the chief conferred with the old woman.

"Sit still, Libby." Jared's voice carried dry amusement. "I'm sure Nick has told you about the curse. The chief thinks it's a shame to get rid of a useful woman. It's true, he finds your fair skin a turn off. Your hair isn't right. Your teeth are too white, and your ears too small. Still, he doesn't like to see me lose a piece of valuable property. He can see you're strong enough. And outsiders have peculiar tastes anyway. So he's asked the medicine woman to work on you."

Libby risked one glance into his eyes, then wished she hadn't. He was obviously enjoying her discomfort.

The old woman came closer, her bracelets jangling. She put a gnarled hand under Libby's chin and raised it till their eyes met.

The *wadian's* eyes were black—deep, deep black. Looking into them, Libby sensed great power. She felt herself sinking into their dark depths. Could this woman *really* know things? She imagined herself opening her soul to the wise old eyes, revealing all her love and longing for Jared.

For a long moment the old woman's eyes burned into hers. Then she dropped her hand and turned back to the chief.

Libby wished desperately that she could understand the conversation that followed. Then from beside her came Nick's whispered words of translation. "She says she's sorry. She can't lift the curse. It's too heavy. But it's not as this man says. There is one who can touch this woman without being doomed. He is the man to whom she has given her heart. No other will ever have her."

179

He paused for a moment. "Now Jared is thanking the chief. They'll be bringing food. Remember, just a little of each. And use the right hand."

Libby nodded. Her heart was hammering in her throat. How had the old woman known so much? Known of her love for Jared? Could she really have seen into Libby's soul?

As the women approached with banana leaves laden with rice and other Dayak delicacies, Libby set her mind to working some complicated mathematical problems. Whatever was in this food—and by now she knew it could be just about anything—she was obliged to eat it.

Their ceremonious dining completed, Jared rose and the others with him. Silently Libby watched the farewells between Jared and the chief. Silently she followed the others down the ladder and through the crowded village to where the *longbots* waited.

There stood an exuberant Njo. "See!" he cried. "Njo get new *mandau*."

Libby smiled. The weapon looked like sword, ax and machete all in one. It seemed to be made of bronze.

As she settled into her seat Njo passed it to her. "You see."

Holding it carefully, Libby examined it. The ebony handle resembled a human head, and from its scalp hung a lock of human hair.

Njo climbed in beside her and took it from her. He swung it in a wide arc. "Cut off heads."

Libby nodded. "I see."

"Enough fun," said Jared dryly, taking his seat in

front of her. "Put that thing away, Njo. Time to get going."

"Okay, boss. Njo go now."

Libby turned to look back as the *longbot* pulled away. Women on the shore were waving, one eye on the departing boats, the other on the naked brown-skinned babies splashing in the shallows.

They were several more hours up river before Jared called a halt for the night. Those hours had passed swiftly for Libby. She was sunk deeply in thought. Why had Jared used that telltale word "doomed"? If he didn't love her at all, he could just have said "cursed." But he had said the man who touched her was doomed to fall under her spell forever. Could that mean that he still loved her?

Her heart pounded in her throat. She had to confront him with this tonight. Tomorrow would be too late. Tomorrow they would reach Longpahanghai, and she felt instinctively that Jared would disappear as soon as he could.

She did her share of setting up camp, did it routinely and automatically, her mind busily seeking ways of making Jared admit to loving her. But no brilliant ideas came.

They ate the usual fish and rice amid jokes about the fine food soon to come, then lingered around the campfire. There was a tinge of sorrow in the air. Libby felt it, and she knew the others did, too. They were a team, now, a team with a job well done. Now they would have to split up. She blinked back sudden tears. She was going to miss Nick and Tim. As for Jared, she couldn't think of being separated from him. She just couldn't.

Finally they all settled down to sleep. But sleep was long in coming to Libby. Jared had left her no opportunity—no opportunity at all—to speak to him.

She woke with the first light of dawn, opening her eyes to see Jared stealing off toward the river. The others were still asleep. Silently she got to her feet and stole after him. The jungle morning was beautiful, rich with the wild beauty she had learned to love. But this morning Libby saw little of it. Her mind was on the man moving silently ahead of her. How could she make him admit to the love she hoped he felt?

Without even a glance around, Jared dropped his *kain* and slid into the water. Libby paused on the bank, then dropped hers and followed him. He was some distance ahead of her and still unaware of her presence. She matched her stroke to his, and when he slowed she slid silently underwater.

In the dim greenness she drew closer, making out his strong muscular legs, the fine hair on them moving gently in the current. An overwhelming tenderness possessed her, and without thinking she reached out to caress him.

His legs exploded in a kick that caught her a glancing blow on the side of the jaw. As unconsciousness grabbed at her, her mouth opened automatically. The ingestion of river water stirred her hazy mind, and with the last of her strength she flailed toward the surface.

"What the hell!" An angry Jared was paddling there. She saw that much as she took a great gasping breath. Then, just as darkness and the water tried to claim her again, she felt his hand in her hair. He rolled her onto her back and set out for shore.

Libby did not try to help him. She relaxed and concentrated on breathing. By the time they had reached the bank, she was nearly herself again. Still, she made no protest when he picked her up and carried her ashore.

He deposited her on a sandy bank and knelt beside her. "Are you all right?" he asked, his eyes wide with concern.

She felt her jaw gingerly. "Yes, Jared. I'm OK."

"That was a damn fool thing to do!" His voice trembled with anger. And maybe, Libby thought, with fear.

"I know," she said humbly. "I wasn't thinking."

He didn't seem to hear her apology. "I could have killed you!"

She reached out to touch his bare chest, her fingers parting the wet, dark hair. "But you didn't. Really, I'm all right. I'm strong, you know."

He shook his head, his gaze on the river. "If I'd knocked you out—you could have sunk right to the bottom"

"Jared!" She grabbed his arm. "Stop it. You didn't hurt me."

Finally he looked down at her. "You never should have come into the jungle."

Anger gave her new strength. "So we're back to that again, are we? Well, Jared, you're wrong. I'm perfectly capable of taking care of myself. In the jungle and elsewhere. You've said so. Remember?"

There was such a look of worry on his face, she knew he must feel *something* for her.

The anger left Libby. She took her heart in her hands. It was now or never. "Jared, do you love me?"

A sharp spasm of pain crossed his face, and he shook his head.

"Jared. I think you do. Just now, when you thought you'd hurt me, I saw it in your face."

Stubbornly he shook his head. "I'd feel concern for any human being."

"Of course you would. But I saw more than that."

Still his jaw remained stubbornly set.

"Jared," she pleaded. "How can I prove that I love you? Tell me. Tell me anything. You want me to dive out of a tree into your arms?" She pushed herself to a sitting position. "The job's over now. Let's do it." She started to get to her feet.

"Libby, stop it. It's still a fool thing to do."

"I don't care," she cried, the tears rising to her eyes. "I want to prove myself to you."

She got to her feet and began to run toward a nearby banyan at the water's edge. She *would* prove it to him, she thought frantically.

"Libby! Stop!"

He was right behind her, his feet in the shallow water, when she reached the banyan. She managed to get up on one branch before his hand closed around her ankle. With a quick jerk he yanked her out of the tree. She fell against his chest. She heard the sharp explosion of his breath as her body slammed into him. They they were both falling, down into the shallows.

Her breath was knocked from her body, but she still struggled. Her dazed mind held only one thought. She had to prove her love to him before it was too late.

Her flailing fists had almost broken his grasp, but

then his hold on her tightened, and he lurched to his feet, dragging her out of the water. Since she was still trying to escape him, he pushed her down on the sandy bank and pinned her there with his body.

"Libby, cut it out!"

She lay struggling under his weight. Her breasts heaved in her efforts to get her breath. "Jared, please. Let me do it."

He had pinned her wrists to the ground or she would have beat at him. "I've got to show you!"

"Libby, be reasonable."

She shook her head, only half conscious of the weight of his body. "I don't want to be reasonable! I love you!" The words were a wail. She discarded her pride. "I've always loved you, Jared. You and no one else." She shuddered convulsively. "All those years" —the tears were coming now—"there's been no one else. You were always there. Always in the way."

A strange expression crossed his face as he gazed down at her. Now Libby grew aware of the feel of his body against hers. All her senses were heightened; she was one enormous longing for him. "Jared! I can't go on like this. I want a husband. A family. Please! Oh, please!" The last word was a moan. "Tell me how I can convince you. Anything. I'll do anything."

"Libby!" The full weight of his body came down on hers as he buried his face in her neck. "Why couldn't you leave well enough alone?" he mumbled. "I was doing OK. I was managing. Finally." He gave a great groan as his hands cradled her wet head, and he raised himself to look into her eyes. "Don't you see, Libby? I'm afraid. I'm afraid to love you. I almost died when you left me. I can't risk that again."

"But, Jared—" She reached up to kiss his chin, wrapped her arms around his broad back. "I'm not going to leave you." Her smile was shaky, but it was a smile. "I've made up my mind. I'm going to follow you. Everywhere. Until you take me back." Her eyes pleaded with him. "Oh, Jared. Darling. I love you so much."

He kissed her fiercely, savagely, and she responded with all the love inside her.

"Please, Jared," she begged when he released her mouth and buried his face between her trembling breasts. "Please say we can try again. Any way you want it."

He groaned again, his mouth against her flesh. "Libby, I'm afraid."

"I know." She stroked his wet hair as she would have a child's. "Me, too. But we're together. We know more now. We know how important our love is. This time we'll make it work." Her laugh was soft. "We have to. We've spoiled each other for anyone else."

He gave a great shudder and she clasped his body to her.

"Did you really mean that?" he asked, his face still against her breast.

"Mean what?"

"That there's been no one else. All these years."

"Yes, I meant it."

"But I thought—"

Her hand stroked his bare back. "You were always there," she said. "Always there in my mind. No man could compete with you."

"Libby—" His words were muffled. "I haven't—"

"I know," she said softly. "I don't blame you. I

186

don't blame you for cheating on me before. I treated you terribly."

There was a long silence. "I didn't cheat on you," he said. "I never would have. That's why it hurt so badly when I thought you had. I thought your accusations were a cover-up for what you were doing."

"No, Jared." She kissed his strong throat. "I was young and stupid. And so afraid of losing you. I couldn't believe it when you left me like that. I sat up all night—waiting for you to come back."

"I did," he said, and his voice reflected his pain. "I came back at noon the next day, but you'd already pulled out."

"Oh, Jared! I should have followed you to the field," she whispered, her lips against his ear. "I let my mother poison my mind."

His lips traced the curve of her cheek, hovered over her mouth. "That's all in the past," he said. "We'll talk it all through and then we'll bury it. We have a future to get on with."

"Oh, Jared, yes!" Her lips sought his frantically, avidly, as she pressed herself against him.

Tim, spying their entwined bodies as he approached, smiled knowingly and retraced his steps to camp. It looked like Libby was going to become a permanent member of the crew—and he couldn't think of anything he'd like more.

Silhouette Desire 15-Day Trial Offer

A new romance series that explores contemporary relationships in exciting detail

Six Silhouette Desire romances, free for 15 days! We'll send you six new Silhouette Desire romances to look over for 15 days, absolutely free! If you decide not to keep the books, return them and owe nothing.

Six books a month, free home delivery. If you like Silhouette Desire romances as much as we think you will, keep them and return your payment with the invoice. Then we will send you six new books every month to preview, just as soon as they are published. You pay only for the books you decide to keep, and you never pay postage and handling.

YOU'LL BE SWEPT AWAY
WITH SILHOUETTE DESIRE

$1.75 each

1 ☐ CORPORATE AFFAIR
James

2 ☐ LOVE'S SILVER WEB
Monet

3 ☐ WISE FOLLY
Clay

4 ☐ KISS AND TELL
Carey

5 ☐ WHEN LAST WE LOVED
Baker

6 ☐ A FRENCHMAN'S KISS
Mallory

7 ☐ NOT EVEN FOR LOVE
St. Claire

8 ☐ MAKE NO PROMISES
Dee

9 ☐ MOMENT IN TIME
Simms

10 ☐ WHENEVER I LOVE YOU
Smith

$1.95 each

11 ☐ VELVET TOUCH
James

12 ☐ THE COWBOY AND THE
LADY   Palmer

13 ☐ COME BACK, MY LOVE
Wallace

14 ☐ BLANKET OF STARS
Valley

15 ☐ SWEET BONDAGE
Vernon

16 ☐ DREAM COME TRUE
Major

19 ☐ LOVER IN PURSUIT
James

20 ☐ KING OF DIAMONDS
Allison

21 ☐ LOVE IN THE CHINA SEA
Baker

22 ☐ BITTERSWEET IN BERN
Durant

23 ☐ CONSTANT STRANGER
Sunshine

24 ☐ SHARED MOMENTS
Baxter

25 ☐ RENAISSANCE MAN
James

26 ☐ SEPTEMBER MORNING
Palmer

27 ☐ ON WINGS OF NIGHT
Conrad

28 ☐ PASSIONATE JOURNEY
Lovan

29 ☐ ENCHANTED DESERT
Michelle

30 ☐ PAST FORGETTING
Lind

31 ☐ RECKLESS PASSION
James

32 ☐ YESTERDAY'S DREAMS
Clay

Silhouette Desire

38 □ SWEET SERENITY
Douglass

39 □ SHADOW OF BETRAYAL
Monet

40 □ GENTLE CONQUEST
Mallory

41 □ SEDUCTION BY DESIGN
St. Claire

42 □ ASK ME NO SECRETS
Stewart

43 □ A WILD, SWEET MAGIC
Simms

44 □ HEART OVER MIND West

45 □ EXPERIMENT IN LOVE Clay

46 □ HER GOLDEN EYES Chance

47 □ SILVER PROMISES Michelle

48 □ DREAM OF THE WEST
Powers

49 □ AFFAIR OF HONOR James

50 □ FRIENDS AND LOVERS
Palmer

51 □ SHADOW OF THE
MOUNTAIN Lind

52 □ EMBERS OF THE SUN
Morgan

53 □ WINTER LADY Joyce

54 □ IF EVER YOU NEED ME
Fulford

55 □ TO TAME THE HUNTER
James

56 □ FLIP SIDE OF YESTERDAY
Douglass

57 □ NO PLACE FOR A WOMAN
Michelle

58 □ ONE NIGHT'S DECEPTION
Mallory

59 □ TIME STANDS STILL
Powers

60 □ BETWEEN THE LINES
Dennis

***LOOK FOR GAMEMASTER
BY STEPHANIE JAMES
AVAILABLE IN JUNE AND
A KISS REMEMBERED BY ERIN ST. CLAIRE
IN JULY.***

SILHOUETTE DESIRE, Department SD/6
1230 Avenue of the Americas
New York, NY 10020

Please send me the books I have checked above. I am enclosing $_____
(please add 50¢ to cover postage and handling. NYS and NYC residents please add
appropriate sales tax.) Send check or money order—no cash or C.O.D.'s please.
Allow six weeks for delivery.

NAME _____

ADDRESS _____

CITY _____ STATE/ZIP _____

Silhouette Intimate Moments

Coming Soon

Dreams Of Evening by Kristin James

Tonio Cruz was a part of Erica Logan's past and she hated
him for betraying her. Then he walked back into her life and
Erica's fear of loving him again was nothing compared to her
fear that he would discover the one secret link that still bound
them together.

Once More With Feeling by Nora Roberts

Raven and Brand—charismatic, temperamental, talented.
Their songs had once electrified the world. Now, after a
separation of five years, they were to be reunited to create
their special music again. The old magic was still there, but
would it be enough to mend two broken hearts?

Emeralds In The Dark by Beverly Bird

Courtney Winston's sight was fading, but she didn't need her
eyes to know that Joshua Knight was well worth loving. If
only her stubborn pride would let her compromise, but she
refused to tie any man to her when she knew that someday he
would have to be her eyes.

Sweetheart Contract by Pat Wallace

Wynn Carson, trucking company executive, and Duke
Bellini, union president, were on opposite sides of the
bargaining table. But once they got together in private, they
were very much on the same side.